SUN IN THE MORNING

Elizabeth Cadell

Large Type
Fic
Cadell

Chivers Press • Thorndike Press
Bath, Avon, England • Thorndike, Maine USA

This Large Print edition is published by Chivers Press, England, and by Thorndike Press, USA.

Published in 1996 in the U.K. by arrangement with the author's estate.

Published in 1996 in the U.S. by arrangement with Brandt & Brandt Literary Agents, Inc.

U.K. Hardcover ISBN 0–7451–4785–2 (Chivers Large Print)
U.K. Softcover   ISBN 0–7451–4793–3 (Camden Large Print)
U.S. Softcover   ISBN 0–7862–0606–3 (General Series Edition)

The text of this Large Print edition is unabridged.
Other aspects of the book may vary from the original edition.

Set in 16 pt. New Times Roman.

Printed in Great Britain on acid-free paper.

British Library Cataloguing in Publication Data available

Library of Congress Cataloging-in-Publication Data

Cadell, Elizabeth.
   Sun in the morning / Elizabeth Cadell
     p. cm.
   ISBN 0–7862–0606–3 (lg. print : lsc)
   1. Large type books.   I. Title.
  [PR6005.A225S86   1996]
  823′.914—dc20

                                    95–43263

To My Two Sisters

CHAPTER ONE

The city of Calcutta, in the year nineteen hundred and thirteen, boasted many fine residential districts, but Minto Lane was not one of them. It began promisingly. It turned off Park Street, and if it had turned south all might have been well. But Minto Lane went north and lost caste as it went.

Five houses stood on it, all of the same design. We lived in the upper story of Number Two and were newcomers to the district. Seated on the floor of our back veranda, my legs dangling through the wooden railings, I had an unrestricted view of the backs of the other houses. Two of them did not matter. Number Three was unoccupied and Number One, on my left, was what was known as a chummery, being occupied by bachelors who looked, to my ten-year-old eyes, elderly and uninteresting. It was to Number Four that my eyes went most frequently and to which in the end I transferred the whole of my interest.

The De Souzas lived at Number Four. The family consisted of a widowed Eurasian mother and eight children, the four eldest of whom were girls and the four youngest, boys. Anybody with a sense of rhythm who cares to run over the names of the De Souzas will understand something of the fascination they were beginning to exercise upon me. Beginning with the eldest and working downwards, they were called Milly, Tutu, Queenie, Cuckoo, Pijjy, Benny, Chum, and Nikko. They were uniformly thin and dark. The girls wore shapeless cotton dresses, the boys, khaki shirts and shorts and tennis shoes which, when new, were white. The youngest boy, Nikko, was about my own age; Milly, the eldest, was seventeen.

They appeared to be a musical family. From their drawing room, which was at the front of the house and therefore invisible from our veranda, came an almost continuous sound of scales played on a tinny piano. My father, who believed me to be a budding virtuoso, envied wistfully the unseen power which kept the pianist at the instrument hour after hour. But the De Souzas did not supply a feast for the ears only. In the largest room of the ground floor sat Mrs de Souza, surrounded by a dozen dirzees all seated cross-legged upon the floor, stitching busily or turning the handles of sewing machines. Round the walls hung garments of brilliant color and varied design, for Mrs de Souza was dressmaker to the Rogers Theatrical Company.

The De Souzas' routine soon became as familiar to me as our own. Their mealtimes were not the same as ours; we kept the English hours—breakfast at eight, lunch at one. They had a small breakfast at half past six and a

2

large breakfast of curry and rice in the Anglo-Indian fashion at eleven. I noted that their ways were not always our ways: they ate curry every day; they ate fruit without either removing the skin or washing it in permanganate of potash; they bought sweets and cakes from Indian peddlers. They did not go for morning walks and seemed to take very little exercise of any kind.

These details I found out for myself, for I was the only member of our household who had the smallest interest in the family of De Souza. My two sisters—aged thirteen and fourteen—were at that time busy with other things. But I was free to pursue a course upon which I was determined—to become acquainted with the De Souzas.

It was a difficult project and there would be bridges to cross, but I felt certain of a welcome at the other end, for the De Souzas, pleased by the interest I showed in them, had begun to stare back. Sometimes as many as five of them together lined their veranda and looked across at me with calm and detached curiosity. 'If you can come,' they seemed to say, 'we shall be glad to see you.'

I thought for a time that I should have to go alone. I felt that there was nobody else who would care to come with me, but I was wrong. Not far away was somebody who was almost as interested in the De Souzas as I was—Poopy Delacourt.

CHAPTER TWO

Poopy Delacourt lived at Minto Lodge and was the only daughter of an extremely silly mother and a brilliant father who was a member of the Indian Civil Service. His daughter's name was Poupée, and for the first eight years of her life she had been called by it. But at eight Poupée was brought to India, and the servants, willing to do their best in English, drew the line at French. They got as near as they could; Poupée became Poopy and remains Poopy to this day. She had no other name, so that there was nothing to fall back upon. In spite of Mrs Delacourt's efforts, Poopy it was, Poopy it had to remain.

We had known the Delacourts for some time. My father liked Mr Delacourt and saw a great deal of him during his wife's frequent visits to England. As Poopy always went with her, our friendship had a slow start; but now we met every day. My sisters and I had joined the Swimming Club and Poopy was already an enthusiastic member.

There were not many lady members. I think we can claim to have been almost the first. Gentlemen had the use of the club until nine every morning. At five minutes to nine my sisters and I sat with Poopy in the little outer office swinging our legs impatiently and

4

inciting the retired sergeant-in-charge to violence.

'Oh, go *on*, Sergeant, do go and tell them to hurry. Look, it's four minutes to, and one of them's still in the water! I can hear him!'

The sergeant, caressing the long waxed ends of his moustache, looked over the swing door and made his report. 'Nobody's in the water, young ladies. They're all out.'

'Then what's that splashing?'

'Well, he's just got out. There now—in a little while you can go in.'

We went in at nine and stayed in the water until half past twelve. On most mornings we had the place to ourselves. At half past twelve another male session began. The sergeant rang the big bell, blew a whistle, clanged the bell again, shouted over the swing door, railed at our ayahs for being unable to exert any authority, clanged the bell again, grew purple blowing the whistle, and finally threatened to put the matter before the committee. At this we came out, and Poopy and I were rubbed down by our ayahs. My sisters scorned any assistance. Struggling into our garments, sipping weak cocoa and nibbling dry biscuits, the twelve-year-old Poopy and I gradually became friends.

I had from the first to put up with my sisters' criticism, for they never understood what I saw in Poopy. The first of many arguments developed after they had refused her offer of a

5

lift home from the Swimming Club in the Delacourts' carriage. Poopy drove away and we crossed the sweltering Strand Road to wait under the shade of the trees for the tram which was to take us home.

'Why couldn't we have gone with her?' I asked, indignantly.

'Because there wasn't room.'

'Yes, there was. She and you two and me...'

'And her ayah and our ayah. You can't leave them behind. At least, you could, but Mrs Delacourt wouldn't like Poopy's to be left behind. Poopy! What a name!'

'People,' I said, 'can't help what their name is. I like her.'

'How can you like her? She's short and fat like a barrel, and look at her clothes! Falling off her! How does she get them like that?'

'Her clothes,' I said, 'are...'

'Oh, they're all *right*. I didn't say there was anything the matter with her clothes—it's what she *does* to them. And her face!'

'I like her face. I think she's got a pretty face,' I said.

'What's pretty about it?' my sisters wanted to know. 'It's got no expression—it's the same all the time and it never changes. You can't tell whether she's pleased or whether she's cross or whether she's...'

'I *can* tell,' I asserted with truth. '*I* can tell, even if you can't. *I* know when she's pleased and when she's...'

6

'Then you're very clever, but you're only saying it because you're sticking up for her.'

'I'm not!'

'Well, if she's your friend, you ought to be.'

'Well, I am, then!'

'You said you weren't!'

'I said...'

The intricacies of the dialogue were put to an end by the arrival of the tram. I climbed into the front seat and sat beside the ayah, acknowledging to myself the truth of my sisters' accusations. Poopy was indeed short and round; her clothes, well-made, expensive, fresh each morning, seemed to disintegrate as the hours went by. Her ayah always carried a store of safety pins with which to fasten the rents and gaps which appeared as the day advanced. I had to acknowledge, too, that Poopy's expression rarely changed, but I was beginning to read her face and I found it far from expressionless. I was thankful for the tram's arrival, for it had prevented my sisters from touching upon the subject of Poopy's hair, which was fair and lank and worn in plaits round her head. As soon as it was tied, strands of hair escaped and stood up in odd little tufts. I knew it could not be long before my sisters said that she looked like an Indian brave whose head feathers had moulted.

Poopy and I became close friends. We had a good deal of time on our hands, for there was at this time something of a gap in our

7

education. Poopy, shuttling between England and India, was accustomed to these gaps. Her mother, she told me, was going to wait until after the holidays, which were now imminent, and then send her to school, which school Poopy neither knew nor cared. By my own parents the matter was felt to be more urgent and my father had put the merits of various establishments before us. There was the Diocesan Girls' School, the Convent in Middleton Row, the small school run by a lady in Park Street, or a larger private school in Chowringhee. My sisters strenuously opposed every one he mentioned and it looked like an impasse until it was found that their objections were not to any school in particular but to education in general.

My sisters and I were certainly happy. On the score of health, well-meaning friends might have scored a point, for we were a weedy trio. I don't think that our combined weights would have added up to that of one hearty, English-bred child. We were small but well-proportioned. Only when we stood against more ample young ladies did we appear as underfed waifs or dainty little dolls, according to the point of view.

Though the question of a school was in abeyance, we continued to learn from our home instructor. My father was a born coach, and it was as well that there were three of us to take the weight of his efforts to turn us into what my mother called general specialists. My father, giving in reluctantly to her view that we couldn't all be good at everything, worked hard to make each of us good at something. The more buoyant of my sisters lay face downward on the music stool while he read out instructions from a book entitled *The New Crawl Stroke*. Arms and legs waving, she made an odd picture on land and an impressive one in the water. Poopy and I stood admiringly on the edge of the swimming pool watching her cut a swift way down its length, while my other sister held a stop watch and yelled encouragement.

'She swims nicely, doesn't she?' said Poopy.

'Yes, a bit.'

Poopy waited until the timing was over and dived with a distressing flop into the water. I joined her and we turned onto our backs, floating lazily. It seemed a good moment to broach a subject I had had in mind for some time.

'Poopy!'

'What?'

'From your back veranda do you ever look at those other houses—Four and Five?'

'I don't like Number Five,' said Poopy, who had a way, which I admired very much, of coming straight to the point. 'I like Number Four.'

'So do I. Do you know who they are?'

'No, but they're called the De Souzas.

They're dark.'

'They're nice, I think. I—I'd like to talk to them.'

'Why don't you then?' inquired Poopy.

I swam to the side, hung on to it, and looked at her.

'I can't go to see them,' I pointed out, 'because I don't know them.'

'Would your mother mind?' asked Poopy, still on her back.

'Well no, I don't think she would, in a way. Would yours?'

'Yes. But I wouldn't tell her,' said Poopy.

I was not surprised. I had spent an afternoon with Poopy at the Minto Lodge flat, and brought away impressions that made my sisters open their eyes and drew a sharp reprimand from my mother.

'I won't have you speaking of Mrs Delacourt in that way!'

'But it's true, Mummy—it really is! I don't know how Poopy can bear it. Her mother *looks* nice and she wears lovely clothes, but she's so *silly*, Mummy. She says silly things to that little dog she's got, and she says silly things to me, and most of the time she keeps on saying "Don't do this" and "Don't do that" to Poopy, and calling her her pet, and I don't wonder Poopy doesn't take any notice.'

With little opposition to fear from Mrs Delacourt, Poopy and I put our heads together and tried to think of a way in which we could meet the De Souzas. Without being able to put it into words, I had a feeling that I would be in a stronger position if I made their acquaintance first and told my family afterwards. The chief stumbling blocks were our ayahs; they accompanied us everywhere and they were impossible to shake off. Mine was much more officious than Poopy's. Her name was Kariman and she had been in my mother's service since my eldest sister was born. My sisters had long ago escaped from her policing. She was now my bodyguard and shuffled after me wherever I went, her earrings swinging, her nose rings twitching with suspicion. Poopy's ayah was fatter than Kariman and lazier. She carried a small wicker stool. Each time we halted, she placed the stool on the ground and sank onto it with a thankful sigh.

'We'll never,' I told Poopy, 'get rid of them.'

Poopy was silent. Anybody else would have thought that she was staring blankly at the fern tubs near which we were standing, but I knew that she was thinking deeply.

'What I think is,' she said at last, 'is to do it one day with Mr Rogers.'

'Do what?'

'Don't you know Mr Rogers?' asked Poopy in surprise.

It was my turn to look astonished. Who did not know Mr Rogers? He was manager, producer, male lead of the Rogers Theatrical Company.

'Who doesn't know him?' I asked.

'Well,' said Poopy, 'hasn't he just come to live next door to you at the chummery?'

I stared at her, puzzled. 'What's that got to do with...'

'He doesn't only act,' said Poopy. 'He goes to see about the costumes, too.'

I suddenly saw what she meant. If he went to see about the costumes, he had to see Mrs de Souza.

'But when ...?'

It was difficult to decide when or even how, but we had not long to ponder. Two evenings later when Poopy and I were playing checkers on our front veranda, Mr Clavering, one of the members of the chummery next door, called on my mother. With him came Mr Rogers. He promised us a box for the new show which was now ready—with the exception of the costumes. He was going along, he told us, to see the dressmaker, Mrs de Souza, to find out whether she could let him have them earlier than the date arranged.

When he rose to go, I looked across at Poopy. She was already on her feet, murmuring her farewell and thanking my mother for having her. When Mr Rogers went down the stairs, Poopy was on one side of him and I was on the other.

We walked to the gate and turned with him to the left. There was a cry from behind and we turned to find Kariman, closely followed by

Poopy's ayah, hurrying to catch up with us.

I addressed them both in Hindustani. 'Go away,' I said. 'We're going along with this gentleman.'

'That's right,' said Mr Rogers in hearty English. 'That's right, old girls. The little what-you-may-call-'em—the little Missy-babas are coming with me. They'll be all right, *mallum?* You pop off—you *jow*, old girls, and I'll bring the Missy-babas back safe and sound. *Mallum?*'

Apparently they *mallumed*. Poopy's ayah sank onto her stool and Kariman, with low growls of suspicion, took up a position by our gate.

We marched on, De Souza bound. Mr Rogers looked down at us. 'Coming to see the costumes, eh?' he inquired.

We looked up at him but said nothing.

Mr Rogers tried again. 'Good dressmaker, this Mrs Whatnot,' he confided. 'I don't know how she turns out the work she does, with all those children—a round dozen, they look like—falling all over the place. There was an old woman who lived in a shoe, what?'

We made no reply. We had turned the corner. The veranda of Number Four was in view. I looked up. Three heads were showing over the railing. We entered the gate and I glanced up once more. Five heads.

The workroom in the lower flat was closed. We crossed the entrance hall and began the ascent of the stairs; Mr Rogers went first and we followed close behind. As in all the Minto Lane houses, the stairs led directly up into a large drawing room and as we mounted I looked up and saw six De Souzas waiting. Mr Rogers reached the top and ran his eye down the line.

'Mrs de Souza in?' he inquired.

'Yes, she's in,' replied one of the girls absently. Nobody was looking at the tall, well-known figure; all eyes were fixed upon Poopy and me. We said 'Good evening' very politely.

Nobody replied, but the same girl put a question. 'What's you-all's names?' she asked.

We told her and went back to staring.

'Mrs de Souza in?' inquired Mr Rogers once more.

One of the boys addressed me. 'I know where you come from,' he stated. 'Often we see you. You live over there'—he waved a hand—'in Number Two, isn't it? But this one'—he drew the attention of his brothers and sisters to Poopy—'she comes from another place.'

'Minto Lodge,' said Poopy apologetically.

'Yes, I thought that's where,' said the boy. 'My name's Benny, and these...'

'I say,' broke in Mr Rogers, 'could you...'

'Wait on, man,' admonished Benny. 'Wait on. See, nobody knows whose names are what. This is Nikko,' he went on, indicating a younger boy, 'and he—that one there—he's

14

Pijjy. And that girl's Cuckoo and that's Queenie. Tutu's shy, she won't come out, and Milly's with my mother and...'

'Well,' interposed Mr Rogers swiftly, 'could you go and tell your mother...'

Benny gave him a second's attention. 'Siddown,' he invited. 'Siddown on that chair and my mother will come.' His eyes came back to me. 'Where do you-all go to school?' he asked.

Mr Rogers, taking matters into his own hands, moved round the room, stopping at each curtained doorway and raising his voice. 'Mrs de Souza! Ho there, Mrs de Souza! Are you ... Oh, there you are!'

Mrs de Souza appeared in a doorway; behind her came a tall thin girl who, I thought, must be Milly. The brown eye appearing round the curtain must belong to the timid Tutu.

Mrs de Souza, fat and smiling, addressed Mr Rogers. 'Oh, Mr Rogers,' she exclaimed, 'you have come to see me?'

Relief overspread Mr Rogers' countenance. 'Ah, Mrs de Souza! I wonder if you could...'

Mrs de Souza's eyes had left his face. She was looking at me, her face shining with honest welcome. 'Oh my!' she exclaimed. 'You are the little girl in the second house, isn't it? I can see you. You sit on your veranda and you hang your legs over, but that is dangerous, as I tell my children, because when the rains come the wood will get rotten and...'

15

Mr Rogers coughed. He was looking less amiable than when we came, and Mrs de Souza hastened to appease him.

'Come. We will go into the veranda,' she said, 'and then there will not be so much noise from the children. Go, go, children,' she instructed. 'Go get lemonade and some sweets.'

There was a convulsive move behind the curtain and I looked towards it. 'Is that Tutu?' I asked.

'Yes. She's so shy,' said Mrs de Souza. 'Come, Tutu,' she urged. 'Come and see these little girls. They...'

She stopped. Mr Rogers was making his way to the head of the stairs. The De Souzas hurried after him and closed round him in explanation and apology. Eight voices were raised in chorus.

'Oh, Mr Rogers, you must think we're so rude, isn't it? First you come to see us, and we talk only to the little girls, but this is the first time...'

Poopy and I stood entranced. The De Souzas used their hands to illustrate each sentence; the gestures were sometimes beautiful, sometimes grotesque. Their shoulders moved; their faces were screwed into an endless variety of grimaces. Mr Rogers looked like a man caught between two streams of traffic, and I thought of the reception he had been accorded at our own house, where he had

16

occupied the center of the stage and talked about himself.

'Come. We will go on to the veranda,' Mrs de Souza promised him. 'Go, children. Benny, go! Go quickly. Tell them to bring Mr Rogers some lemonade.'

Mr Rogers, however, was not eager for the lemonade. All he wanted, he explained in slightly mollified tones, was an assurance that the dresses for the revue would be ready in a fortnight.

There was no difficulty, said Mrs de Souza. The dresses could be ready whenever he wanted them. Mr Rogers thanked her, bowed his farewell, and went downstairs. On the bottom step he turned. Poopy and I were following him and the six youngest De Souzas were following us. Mr Rogers threw me a look of desperate appeal.

I hesitated and then remembered Poopy's ayah and Kariman, waiting for us at our gate. If they saw him pass without us...

I looked up at Mr Rogers and, slipping my hand into his, encircled his thumb in a vicelike grip. 'I'm coming with you,' I said.

I felt sorry for him. I knew that he had no wish to be seen in his present company. Passers-by could see the well-known and popular actor surrounded by a shouting, shabby band of De Souzas. Publicity of that kind could do nothing for Mr Rogers.

He walked to the gate, tight-lipped and

17

silent. Poopy and I were by his side, clinging firmly, and round us were the chattering, gesticulating Queenie, Cuckoo, Pijjy, Benny, Chum, and Nikko. We hurried out of the gate, turned the corner, and passed Number Three at a brisk pace. When I was certain that Kariman had seen us together, I released Mr Rogers. Two seconds later he vanished into the sanctuary of Number One. Poopy, with a farewell word, went home with her ayah.

Kariman rose to her feet, grunted, and inspected my escort. 'Who,' she inquired, 'are all these babas?'

'Mr Rogers' friends.'

Mr Rogers' friends made me an enthusiastic farewell—their voices must have been heard halfway up Park Street. I ran upstairs, ignored my sisters' comments on my new acquaintances, and found my father lying on his favorite lounge in the veranda.

'What was all that halooing out there?' he inquired.

'The De Souzas,' I said.

'And who are the De Souzas?'

Clambering onto an arm of his chair, I told him happily. 'Milly, Tutu, Queenie, Cuckoo, Pijjy...'

CHAPTER THREE

Mrs de Souza was a widow. The family was large, but its members were so individual that it was impossible to get them mixed. Milly, the eldest, was the pianist whose industry my father had praised. Tutu came next—sixteen, and fond, her mother told us, of the men. Queenie and Cuckoo, who were fourteen and fifteen respectively, looked like twins and were inseparable. Like their sisters, they had long black hair which they wore flowing in a way which I thought must be extremely hot. They went to the Convent and hoped that Poopy and I would soon join them there.

All four boys went to St Xavier's College. Three of them were loud and noisy and spent most of their time making kites and flying them. We found the De Souzas a charming family and Benny, we decided, was the nicest of them all.

Benny De Souza was twelve and knew everything. His conversation was an undiluted stream of solid facts. His sources of information were a stock of old geographical magazines, an almanac for the year 1884, and the De Souzas' lean, wizened cook, who claimed to have sailed round the world and learned practically everything in it. What he had learned he was now passing on to Benny, who relayed it to privileged listeners. To hear him reeling out facts in his nasal, singsong voice, with both hands waving, was something of which Poopy and I could never tire. Snubbed in one quarter, Benny took his information to another. Like the rest of his family, he had no malice in his composition and saw none in others. Given an audience, he was contentment itself—a thin, shabby little Eurasian boy who found nothing wrong with anything.

It was Benny who pointed out that Number Three, being empty, would make a very fine playground for us all. We welcomed the suggestion, for it solved the problem of a headquarters. The servants, inaudibly but unmistakably, disapproved of my friendship with the De Souza family. I took no notice of Kariman's outraged mutterings, but it was difficult to brush aside Yusuf, whom we considered a king among bearers. He was a magnificent six-foot-two picture of dignity. He ruled the other servants, ran the house competently, and loved us all as much as he loved his son Ali, who was also in our employ. All our servants looked down their noses at my friendship with the De Souzas.

At Number Three we could avoid all these difficulties. It was cool and spacious; we could play hopscotch on the black and white marble squares of the entrance hall or run in and out of the rooms playing last-touch. No doors were locked; the place was our own. When it was too hot for exertion, we could close the shutters and lie on the cool floors reading or playing snakes-and-ladders; we stopped passing peddlers and bought their doubtful wares—highly colored cakes and Indian sweets dripping with syrup. We bought little paper cones of monkey-nuts, ready cooked. The brown inner skin flaked off crisply between our fingers. I borrowed money from the protesting Kariman and invited snake charmers to give performances in the compound; monkey men shook their noisy rattles and made the monkeys dance for us. The days were long and pleasant—so pleasant that when Benny came one morning with the news that the house had been let, Poopy and I were stricken.

'You mean someone's taken it—all of it?' Poopy asked.

'Not all,' said Benny, wagging his head. 'The downstairs is not let. But upstairs—gone!'

'When are the people coming?' I asked.

'It's taken from now—from at once. I met the babu who works for the landlord and he told me. He said, "Ho, Benny, no more playing in Number Three." Like that, he said. I asked him, I said, "Why no more playing?" and he told me. He said the people are to come in.'

'Which people?' asked Poopy.

Benny's eyes glistened. He gave a sound of glee, stood on his hands for a few moments, and, righting himself, addressed us. 'Guess who!' he said.

'Well, who?' asked Poopy irritably. 'How can we guess? I don't know how many people there are in Calcutta'—she raised her voice to drown Benny's as he began to tell her—'and I don't care, but it's too many to guess. Who, Benny?'

Benny leaned forward and spoke in an awed tone. 'Mr Andros!' He waited for our reactions, but they were disappointing.

Poopy and I merely stared blankly. 'Who?'

'Mr Andros. Mr *Andros*,' repeated Benny. 'You don't know? My goodness, man, you haven't heard of Mr Andros?' His voice was an incredulous squeak.

'No, we haven't. Who is he?' demanded Poopy.

'Everybody knows him,' said Benny. 'He's that chap that goes and shoots man-eaters.'

'Man-eaters?'

'Yes. Leopards, but mostly tigers. Tigers,' proceeded Benny, fixing us with a steady look, 'don't eat people. They aren't man-eaters, not in their nature, but only when they get hurt. When they get hurt, and when they get ill, and when they can't kill properly in the jungle, then they have to eat something, isn't it? So they eat men. They turn into man-eaters and they go into the villages softly, softly...' Benny, carried away by his own eloquence, raised himself on tiptoe and came creeping towards us. Poopy and I retreated. 'They go and they catch a man and they carry him off and crunch him up. And a woman, also. And then they go on eating because they like the taste and when they eat a good many, the chaps in the village get very frightened and they say, "This tiger'll eat us all up if we don't watch." And they say, "All right then. We'll send a message to Andros Sahib, and Andros Sahib will come and shoot—bang-bang—and then no more man-eater." All over India, I'm telling you, they know Mr Andros. They...'

'Yes,' broke in Poopy, 'but has he got any girls or boys?'

Benny put his head on one side and considered. 'No,' he said at last, 'I don't think so, but I'll ask the babu. I'll ask him today if I see him.'

The news on the following day was a little better. Benny reported that Mr Andros had a wife and daughter. The babu was unable to give the exact age of the daughter, but thought she was about twelve.

'Well, if they're only taking the top flat,' said Poopy, 'perhaps we'll still be able to play downstairs if we let her play with us.'

On this hopeful note the matter rested, but I asked my father if he had ever heard of a Mr Andros and found that he had. Most people, he told me, had heard of him, for he was a brave man, a fine sportsman, and responsible for delivering several villages from the scourge of man-eating tigers.

Other details concerning Mr Andros came to light. He was a Greek and had come to India about fifteen years earlier. He had been twice married. The daughter was the child of the first marriage, Mr Rogers told us.

'What's her name?' I asked.

'Name?' Mr Rogers said. 'Let me see. It's a French kind of one, I remember. Marie? No, not Marie, but it's something like it. Marie, Marie ... I've got it! Marise. That's it, Marise. Wait till you see, young lady. My word, you'll have to pull your socks up! Real French miss, you know.'

I slipped away to acquaint Poopy with the new facts. When we sought out Benny, we found that he could add to our information, for Queenie and Cuckoo, on hearing the name Andros, had revealed that they knew Marise Andros well—at all events, by sight. She went to the Convent; she was not in the same form as Queenie and Cuckoo, but they were able to describe her.

'She's so pretty!' said Cuckoo, on a long breath. 'And she wears such dresses!'

'So many dresses,' broke in Queenie. 'My! How much they cost, I don't know, and she never wears the same. She ...'

'She's got curls—ringlets,' said Cuckoo. 'She ties them up on her head with ribbons, and so pretty she looks!'

She made an attempt to show us but found it difficult, for we were walking across to my house bearing a gift of homemade mango chutney from Mrs de Souza to my mother. I led the way through our drawing room and into a bedroom where my mother sat, pencil in hand, as the laundryman counted piles of washing.

When the laundryman swung the bundle on his back and lifted the curtain to go through the doorway, I saw that Benny was coming up the stairs. He gave a glance at my father seated on the veranda and, after a moment's hesitation, walked out and stood beside his chair.

'Hello,' said my father.

Benny nodded. 'That's a Burma cigar you're smoking?' he asked.

'Yes.'

'A Pegu brand?'

'Yes. How did you know?'

Benny wagged his head without undue conceit. 'I know. I know things. You get them in that shop in Chowringhee near Kyd Street?'

'Quite right.'

'They are not bad,' said Benny, getting into his stride. 'I know about them. At my school I know Daniel Munro, and it is his father's shop where they sell them. His mother is my mother's cousin twice removed. You know twice removed?' he paused to ask.

My father nodded, but Benny thought it as well to make sure. 'Twice removed,' he explained, 'is when you have a cousin and *that* cousin gets married. Then that son is also your cousin, but he is twice removed. You see?'

My father nodded gravely.

'You can be more,' proceeded Benny. 'You can be three times.'

My father nodded once more, and Benny looked a little shaken. It was obvious that he was haunted by a fear that my father knew almost as much as he did. He went nearer and, standing close to my father's chair, put a small brown hand on his arm. My father waited.

'You have been a lot in England?' asked Benny.

'Yes.'

'Then you know everything that is there?'

'Well—no. You see, I only go for a little while, on leave, and I don't have time to—to learn very much.'

Benny's face cleared. He hitched up his shorts, cleared his throat, and took a deep breath. 'I will tell you,' he said. 'I will...'

There was an interruption. From below came a shrill, urgent summons. 'Queenie! Cuckoo! Come, come quickly! Come quickly and bring Benny. Come!'

Benny took three steps and looked over the veranda at a breathless, agitated Tutu standing in the compound below. Queenie and Cuckoo joined him and the three peered over anxiously.

'What's up?' asked Benny.

'Come quickly! Those people have come,' called Tutu. 'All their furniture has been put in already and we didn't see! Now they've come themselves. Come! Come and see!'

Before the last words were out of her mouth, her listeners were halfway down our stairs. I hesitated for a moment and then followed them, wondering whether Poopy knew of the arrival. Before I got to the gate, I saw her coming towards me.

'That new girl—she's come,' she said.

'I know. Tutu told us. Shall we go and see what she's like?'

'Yes, come on,' said Poopy.

We went quickly towards the gate and behind us, agitatedly waving our solar topees, came Poopy's ayah and Kariman. We put the topees on impatiently, walked out into the lane, and joined the entire De Souza family who were lined up, watching every detail of the arrival. Perhaps their undisguised staring made us a little disinclined to stare ourselves, and Poopy and I turned involuntarily in the direction of home. At that moment we heard the sound of swift footsteps and turned back. A girl ran out of the gate, saw us, and stopped to inspect us.

The three of us stood quite still for a few moments. She saw Poopy—fat, untidy, calm, and, in spite of her figure, oddly dignified. She saw me—small, with legs like sticks, with hair scraped back and a topee balanced on my head.

We saw a dainty frock and spotless white

shoes, a rounded little figure, dimpled hands, and ringlets—real, we saw at once—drawn up off the neck and tied in enchanting bunches at each side of the head. And in between the bunches, tilted blue eyes, a small nose, and a Cupid's-bow mouth. And, like a crown on a princess, a solar topee—not a plain white one like Poopy's and mine, but covered with white cotton material with bands of insertion through which were threaded narrow blue ribbons. It was perfection. It was Marise.

Poopy and I engraved the picture permanently on our minds and then turned and walked slowly away. The ayahs followed us reluctantly. They would have liked to stay and stare with the De Souzas. We walked in silence to the gate of my house and then parted.

Poopy put a question. 'Do you like her?'

'Yes. I like her very much. Do you?'

'Yes.'

We both liked her very much. Today—nearly thirty-six years later—we still do.

CHAPTER FOUR

We were now a trio. The De Souzas were our friends and we liked them, but Poopy, Marise, and I fell at once into the peculiar relationship which was to endure for so long. There was scarcely any preliminary. The day after

Marise's arrival we were strolling up Park Street for our early morning walk three abreast, as much at ease as if we had known one another for years.

Behind came Kariman, Poopy's ayah, and a newcomer so grand that one could scarcely call her an ayah. She spoke English, snubbed her two colleagues, and was called Rosie. Marise took no notice of her whatsoever, but Poopy and I both felt that she added something of an air to our promenade. We reached Chowringhee, crossed the road, and found ourselves on the open green of the Maidan.

'Do you come here every morning?' asked Marise.

'No. Sometimes we do and sometimes we stay at home and sometimes we play in your house—at least, we did when it was empty.'

'It's still empty downstairs,' said Marise.

'We can play there. Where do you go to school?'

'Nowhere, yet.'

'Nowhere?' Marise raised her eyebrows.

'Well, Poopy's just come,' I explained, 'and I used to live out at Ballygunge, and I had lessons from somebody else's governess.'

'Tell your mother to send you to the Convent,' directed Marise. 'That's where I go. Then we'll be together.'

'We're not Catholics,' said Poopy. 'Are you?'

'Of course. I'm French,' went on Marise,

'half of me, because my mother was. Her name was Seraphine, but she's dead.'

'I know,' I said, and was surprised to find Marise turning to look at me.

'How do you know?' she asked a little sharply.

'Well, I heard. Somebody who lives next door to us met her once.'

'She was very pretty,' said Marise. 'I know because I've seen photographs. Her name was Seraphine Legrand, and my grandmother and my grandfather live at Chandernagore and I go to see them for a month every Christmas.'

'Don't they ever come here?' asked Poopy.

'Sometimes my grandfather does, but my grandmother's very delicate and she never goes anywhere.'

'Poor thing,' said Poopy.

'Why poor thing? She likes to stay at home,' said Marise. 'She's got a great big house with marble staircases. I'd take you and show you, but she's delicate and so that's why I go by myself, but you'll see my grandfather when he comes.'

We saw him a few days later. He had come to Calcutta on what Marise called official business. We had no idea what this meant but it impressed us, and Mr Legrand impressed us even more. He was a short, spare man but his pointed grey beard, his smart topee, elegant cane, and courtly manners were very imposing, while the fact that he and Marise chattered together in French impressed us most of all. He took leave of us with a stiff bow and hoped that he would meet us again.

Struck by a thought, I addressed Marise eagerly. 'You know, Marise,' I said, 'there's somebody called Mr Clavering next door to us and he takes us for picnics in his launches. You could come and...'

'I don't like going in launches,' said Marise.

'But if we stopped at Chandernagore, you could go and see your grandfather and...'

Marise raised her shoulders. 'I'm going to see him, silly,' she said. 'For a whole month. You could come too, only my grandmother's so delicate, so you can't see how big the house is.'

She broke off to give a twitch to Poopy's dress, which seemed about to come off altogether. I looked from one to the other and wondered at the wide differences in our appearance. It was extraordinary that with the same basic garments we looked so little alike. We each wore a cotton vest onto which was buttoned a pair of cotton knickers. Over this came a pinafore. But though the garments might be the same, the material, the design, the embroidery and effects were vastly different. My pinafores were plain; Poopy's were more elaborate, having lace trimmings and some ribbons which, falling off as the day advanced, left them looking as plain as mine. Marise's were miracles of daintiness; they were shorter than ours and stuck out like ballet skirts, and we could hardly count the rows of lace or of insertion run through with pale blue or pale pink ribbons. Her topee covers were as elaborate and as varied as her pinafores and made a charming frame for her face. In the late afternoon when we had changed into frocks, the number and variety of Marise's could not be counted, and she wore colored kid shoes which Poopy and I thought were the most dashing thing we had ever seen.

Some of the more elaborate dresses were made, she told us, by her grandmother of silks sent from France by Mr Legrand's relations. Grandmother, we found, also made the topee covers.

We accepted Marise as the fashion leader in our small circle. Her comments on our appearance were outspoken and unfavorable, and though I felt that I always looked neat, I could do nothing but agree with her strictures on Poopy. Poopy was a sight.

Marise was the leader in other things besides fashion. She swam better than we did, she was able to rattle off French at a great rate, and she had a delicate grandmother living in a grand house with marble staircases. We got a little tired of the marble staircases but before we had time to tell her so, Fate, in the shape of Mr Clavering's launch, bore us to Chandernagore.

It was on a Sunday morning. I had overslept, and I was awakened by the less gentle of my sisters, who sat on my bed and beat a tattoo on my chest.

'Come on! Wake up!' she shouted. 'Wake up quickly! We're going on a river trip.'

I sat up eagerly. 'All of us?'

Mr Clavering's voice boomed in our drawing room and I ran out in my nightgown to learn the details.

'Come on now, lazybones,' he said. 'You and your sisters. No room for mothers and fathers.'

'Can I take Poopy and Marise?' I asked. 'Will there be room?'

'You can bring Poopy. Who's this Marise? Oh, she's the new one, isn't she?'

'Can she come?'

'She can come. And you've all got to look sharp and get down to Outram Ghat in an hour.'

He hurried downstairs and I leaned over the banisters. 'Have I got to bring Kariman?'

'That fat ayah of yours? No, and not Poopy's old girl with the portable stool, either, and tell that other, what's her name...'

'Marise.'

'Marise. Tell her to leave hers behind, too, if she's got one. Oh, and tell your mother not to bother about food and drink. I've got it all.'

I threw three canfuls of cold water over me in the bathroom, hurried into a clean cotton frock before Kariman had half dried me, and went to fetch Poopy. Together we went round

33

to Number Three, and here disappointment met us. Marise had gone for an early morning walk with her father. They would not be long, but by the time they got back it would be too late to go to the launch.

We turned away. We were already so much a team that the trip without Marise lost much of its charm. We climbed into the foremost gharry and drove with Mr Clavering and Charles Rogers to Outram Ghat. Behind us came my sisters and Mr and Mrs Knox, who lived in the flat below us.

The drive to the Ghat was cool and refreshing, and when we arrived and walked down to the jetty we saw that there were two launches waiting, a large and a small.

'They've brought 'em both, I see,' said Mr Clavering after a glance. 'Well'—he turned to his guests, who now consisted of several people in addition to our own party—'who's for which? We'll let the kids choose. Now then, little 'uns, which'll you have?'

My sisters liked the little one. Poopy and I preferred the lovely large white one and were told to go aboard. We were helped on and made our way to a seat on the deck.

'Let's stay here,' suggested Poopy. 'The breeze'll be nice. Do my back up, will you?'

I walked round and tried to button her dress, but two buttons were missing. 'Did you have them all on when you came out?' I asked.

''Course I did,' said Poopy. 'But they don't

sew them on properly. Have you got a pin?'

'No, I haven't. I could ask someone, though.'

I asked several of the party now assembled on the launch. Nobody could oblige me until I came to Mrs Knox, who not only produced a pin but came and fastened it on.

'We'll have a safety pin, I think,' she said. 'Turn round, Poopy. There! I think that will stay. Do your shoelace up, my dear. That's it. And could you pull up your ... That's right. Will they stay up?'

Poopy thought they might. Mrs Knox returned to the grownups and Poopy and I went to wave to the smaller launch, which was preceding us up the river.

We slid along on the smooth water and a cool breeze blew deliciously. Nobody took any notice of us. We inspected the engine room, leaned perilously over the launch's side, ate bananas, drank iced lemonade, and wished that Marise could have been with us to share the fun.

'But it doesn't matter, really,' I said, 'because we aren't going to stop at Chandernagore, Mr Clavering says.'

We did, however, stop at Chandernagore. Nobody minded very much where the launch pulled in, and Chandernagore was as good a stopping place as any other. We had lost sight, long ago, of the smaller launch. The sun was beating mercilessly down and the breeze was no longer cool. Nobody, when the launch tied up for a short halt, felt the least desire to leave it and walk into the scorching heat of the shore. Even Poopy and I, who had planned to slip away and look at the Legrand residence, hesitated.

'Too hot for landing,' called Mr Clavering from the other side of the deck. Everybody but ourselves was seated in the shade on the side of the launch looking over the river. Poopy and I hung over the hot railing on the other side and looked longingly towards the tiny little town.

'We'll push away in ten minutes,' called Mr Clavering.

Ten minutes wasn't long and it was very hot, but it seemed a pity to lose this opportunity.

'Come on,' said Poopy suddenly.

Nobody saw us go. We went cautiously, for somebody might have noticed us and remembered that we were without our ayahs. The fact gave us a little feeling of excitement. This was almost an adventure!

We came up the jetty, paused, and then hurried along the dusty road.

'It's a big house. It ought to be easy to notice,' I said. 'There aren't many very big houses.'

We walked as far as we dared, fearful that the launch would leave without us, but we found no house that looked in the least like the one Marise had described.

'Let's ask,' I panted. My clothes were

sticking to me and I could feel perspiration trickling down my back.

We stopped a man and asked in Hindustani where Legrand Sahib's house was.

The man pointed instantly to a small road branching down to the river. 'The first house, Miss-Sahib,' he said.

He walked on, and we went down the road he had pointed out. We walked between two gharries standing at the roadside and saw before us the first house. It was a bungalow—sunbaked, shabby, standing in a neat but parched garden. Poopy and I stood and stared at it blankly.

'He told us wrong,' said Poopy.

'Yes.' I was disappointed, but we had to go back.

Then I saw to my surprise that Poopy was looking fixedly at a small board beside the gate. Following her glance, I read the name painted on it: Pierre Legrand. I was still staring at it and trying to clear my thoughts when Poopy caught my arm in a painful grip and dragged me behind one of the gharries.

'Don't let him see you,' she whispered.

'Who?'

'There—look!'

I looked. The wide veranda was unscreened. Beyond, in a drawing room which reminded me of Mrs de Souza's, sat two people, a man and a woman. The man was Mr Legrand—not the trim, elegant Mr Legrand we had seen in

37

Calcutta, but a man more informal, in a cool shirt, taking his ease in the heat of the afternoon, his papers and books by his side, a long drink at his elbow. Beside him, sorting the contents of a workbox, sat a woman—a thin, neat Eurasian woman.

'Come away,' said Poopy.

I obeyed. We drew cautiously away from the gharries, reached the end of the road, and without a word took to our heels and ran as fast as we could towards the landing stage. We ran until I could scarcely draw a breath and then broke into a shambling trot. My mouth was dry and parched, my clothes perspiration-soaked and sticking to my skin. The glare was appalling, and as I gave my topee a jerk to draw it further over my eyes, the elastic under my chin snapped and the topee rolled in the dust. I picked it up, put it on my head, and hurried along, holding it awkwardly. As we neared the river, I became panic-stricken at the thought that the launch had left without us. I threw a glance at Poopy. Her expression was as blank as usual, but the state to which our haste had reduced her clothes slowed me down and I addressed her as well as my lack of breath would allow.

'P-Poopy, you're coming all undone.'

'It doesn't matter,' said Poopy. 'Hurry!'

'Yes, I am, but your back is showing.'

'Well, let it.'

'Oh, but Poopy, your—your Sunday's

below your Monday!'

'Oh, *bother* the things!' Poopy stooped and gave a hitch to garments which were now at so perilous a level that I realized that only one button separated us from total disaster. I could do nothing except long suddenly for the ayah with her stock of safety pins.

The jetty was in sight. At the end of it, to our infinite relief, was the launch, its near deck still empty. We clambered aboard unobserved and sank, hot and breathless, onto two wicker chairs. We had scarcely sat down when we heard Mr Clavering give the order to cast off. The launch moved slowly into midstream and headed towards Calcutta. A breeze, hot and drying, blew on my forehead, on my damp and rumpled clothes, and loosened some of the hair which was clinging to my face and neck.

We sat silent. We had stumbled on an uncomfortable piece of knowledge and we were anxious to push it to the back of our minds. Trying to put myself in Marise's place, I decided that I would have remained silent on the subject, but I had to admit, with deep respect, that I could never have thought up the big house and the big gardens and the marble staircases. That was Marise. I had nothing to say against her way of dealing with the problem and I was certain that Poopy hadn't, either.

The Delacourts' carriage waited at the Ghat, and it was decided that Poopy should take Mr and Mrs Knox and me. My sisters were to follow with Mr Clavering. We drove to our house and Poopy, telling the coachman to wait for her, came into the house with me. We were not surprised to find Marise waiting for us. She leaned over the banisters and came down to meet us.

'Thank you very much for the drive, Poopy,' said Mrs Knox. 'Did you enjoy the river trip? What a pity you couldn't come, Marise.'

'Yes,' agreed Marise. 'Did you stop anywhere?'

'Yes,' said Mrs Knox, 'we stopped for a little while at Chandernagore.'

Marise stared thoughtfully at a safety pin on Poopy's dress. 'Did anybody,' she asked slowly, 'get off the boat?'

'Dear me, no,' said Mrs Knox. 'We were only there for a little while, and it was far too hot to get off. We all sat quietly on board.'

Poopy and I were glad to hear it stated clearly and on the highest authority. Nobody could question Mrs Knox's accuracy.

She paused on her way into her drawing room and turned for a moment. 'I forgot, Marise,' she said. 'Your grandfather lives there, doesn't he?'

'Yes,' said Marise, skipping after her. 'In a big house, with marble staircases and...'

They disappeared through the doorway and I walked with Poopy to the waiting carriage.

'Good-by,' I said. 'I'll see you tomorrow.'

''By,' said Poopy.

That was all that was said of the matter, and it was almost seven years before Poopy and I referred to it again.

CHAPTER FIVE

The fact that Marise attended the Convent made our decision regarding a school a great deal easier. I raised a loud voice in favor of going there, and my father gave his consent.

It was arranged that on the Monday morning after the holidays had ended we were all to go to school at the Convent.

When the day came, I hurried through my breakfast and looked eagerly over the front veranda. At half past eight, I called to my sisters. 'Come on! Come on and hurry up! They're all here, and you're not ready!'

My sisters gave one appalled glance over the veranda and hurried to appeal to my mother. 'Mummy! Oh Mummy, come and look! We haven't got to go with all that lot, Mummy, have we? Oh Mummy, there's a whole crowd and ...'

It was indeed an imposing procession. At the head came Queenie and Cuckoo, dressed alike in shapeless white cotton dresses and white canvas shoes. Behind them was Marise, spotless and dainty, her skirt short and wide

41

and stiffly starched. Poopy stood beside her, one sock already working its way down into her shoe, a hair ribbon already untied. Behind them came Chum and Nikko, each with a bundle of books under one arm. Then came Pijjy and Benny and last, Poopy's ayah, Marise's ayah, and a diminutive bearer carrying Queenie's and Cuckoo's books.

'Mummy, we don't have to walk to school with them, do we? *Look* at them!'

'The boys only go as far as Park Street,' I pointed out. 'Then they go *that* way.'

This was something. My sisters followed me downstairs, leaving a good margin between themselves and the rest of the throng, and Kariman brought up the rear.

At the Convent I found to my dismay that I was to be parted from my friends and relations. My sisters were put into a class above mine; I had expected this, but I had hoped to be with Poopy and Marise. They were older than I was, but I was resolved to work hard to keep up with them.

Poopy and Marise, however, were in the class below mine. Poopy's education had been of a sketchy character. Her mother's moves were so frequent that Poopy had gone into and out of a number of schools in what must have been record timings. Most of Marise's time was spent in watching the clock and wondering when the lesson was to end. Our separation widened as the days went on, for I rose slowly and reluctantly to the top of my class, while Poopy and Marise sank rapidly to the bottom of theirs. They watched my prowess without a trace of envy. A brain, to Poopy and Marise, was something you could be born with or without. If you had one, learning was easy; if you hadn't, it was no use bothering.

We met at noon when the school assembled in the central hall for the Angelus. Then the boarders went to the dining room and the day girls trooped out to a long, stone-floored veranda with trestle tables running along its length. On these our bearers had spread our tiffin and stood waiting, the food kept warm in aluminum tiffin carriers. There was an overpowering smell of curry and oranges.

There was little activity after lunch. The weather was getting cooler, but it was still too hot to go out of doors and run about. We walked up and down the veranda or stood in groups. Our group consisted of Poopy, Marise, and myself and the girls who sat near me in class. There was an Indian girl named Cloma, thin, clever, with sleek black hair oiled and brushed close to her head. There was also Vali, who was the Rajah of Timpari's daughter, tall, beautiful, and reserved.

Cloma's father was one of Calcutta's most brilliant lawyers. He was engaged in an unceasing campaign to throw the British out of India. Cloma seemed to have no feelings on the subject.

Vali was learning the violin and I was very often able to escape from the needlework lesson and sit beside her while she practiced in the music room. It was here that Mother Terasita, the Music Nun, found me so often that her curiosity was aroused.

'Why,' she asked, 'do you come and sit in here?'

'Well, I—I come to listen to Vali, Mother.'

'Are you musical?'

'I think so. I play the piano.'

'Who teaches you?'

'My father.'

'Is he a professor of music?'

'Oh, no! He isn't a—well, he isn't a professor at all. He...'

I paused. It was difficult to explain my father's lack of confidence in music teachers.

'Play me something,' directed Mother Terasita.

I sat down at the piano, wondering what I should play. My repertory was extensive. My father had once, in his more irresponsible days, owned a banjo. He had taught me every cakewalk ever written, and I also knew all the Sousa marches, most of the Strauss waltzes, half the Gilbert and Sullivan operas, and the overture from *William Tell*. These were scarcely suitable. I searched my memory and chose a short mazurka by Chopin. Mother Terasita listened without comment, thanked me, and gave me a note to carry home to my

44

father. Would he, the note read, call and see Mother Terasita at his convenience to discuss the advisability of placing me under the tuition of Miss Inga Gumm?

Miss Gumm had studied the piano at Leipzig and was now studying Indian music in Calcutta. She took no pupils, but Mother Terasita had apparently made up her mind that here was a combination of a unique promise and a unique teacher.

I walked to the Convent with my father and as he went, he gave me his reasons for not giving way to Mother Terasita. He was with her for fifteen minutes. She had a dovelike voice, an angel's face, and the persistence of a bull terrier. On the way home my father gave me his reasons for giving way to Mother Terasita. The thing was settled. I was the pupil, the sole pupil, of Miss Gumm.

I went with my music case to Miss Gumm's flat in Camac Street. I knew her by sight, so that her broad, squat appearance was no surprise to me. Her accent was thick and rich, and the room to which she led me was the nearest thing to a private museum I ever saw. As a den or a study for Mr Andros it would have been highly suitable, for the walls were hung with trophies and the floor was covered with skins; on chairs and on the sofa, even on the edge of the beautiful grand piano, were unmounted heads, each wilder and shaggier than the last.

Miss Gumm pushed aside an elephant's foot and waved me to the piano stool. 'Now,' she said, 'we will blay.'

She put a Chopin study before me. It was one I knew and I began it with confidence, but before I had gone very far I felt a strong push and found Miss Gumm preparing to take my place. I vacated the piano stool and she sat down, crouched low on the stool, and rubbed her hands softly together. Presently she held them above the notes and bent low over the piano, her left ear close to the notes in an attitude of listening. I waited breathlessly for the ear to touch the low G sharp, and at that moment she brought her hands down on the keys and began to play. I forgot her ear, forgot her odd shape and accent and the wild heads and tails all around us. I was listening, for the first time, to a great artist and I sat entranced.

Miss Gumm finished the study, rubbed her hands, bent over the notes, and played two more studies before she remembered me. 'Yes,' she said. 'You will blay well.'

She gave up the stool and allowed me to play several bars of a sonata. Then I was pushed aside and Miss Gumm finished it for me.

When the process had been repeated several times, I looked at a clock half hidden by a boar's head and gave a cry. 'Oh Miss Gumm, look at the time!'

Miss Gumm seemed uninterested in the time, and I learned that my lessons only ended when I packed my music reluctantly in the case, crept to the door, and let myself out. Sometimes I spent two hours with her. She never began a work, for something seemed to tell her that I was a pupil and here to learn. But at the first false note, the first weak passage, I was pushed off the stool and Miss Gumm took over. It was, perhaps, an unorthodox method, but after my first surprise I found nothing wrong with it. All I had to do was to learn to play like Miss Gumm.

CHAPTER SIX

Poopy's mother had a dog named Buffer. Nobody liked Buffer, a highbred, yapping animal given to helping himself to small pieces of any stranger unwary enough to pass close to him. He never accompanied Mrs Delacourt on her visits to us, for my father would not have him in the house. My sisters and I avoided him, as we had been taught to avoid all dogs. One day, my father promised, we should have as many as we liked, but that would be in England where dogs ran little or no risk of rabies. In the meantime we must keep away from them.

On the morning when Buffer dashed down Park Street and swerved along Minto Lane and into our gate, avoidance was impossible. I had just come downstairs, ready for school. I was within a few yards of Poopy and Marise, who were waiting for me. In the gateway were the De Souzas and behind them, Poopy's ayah, stooping to remove a stone from her shoe. The dog ran past her and came to a stop facing us, and we did not need anybody to tell us that he had gone mad.

For a few seconds we all stood as though frozen. Then I saw a flash of white as Yusuf's sleeve came round me and I was snatched up the steps of the entrance. I saw Marise take a step forward. Benny, putting out a hand, gripped her arm and held her still. Kariman, with great good sense, ducked behind a clump of ferns, but Poopy's ayah, braver and more foolish, rushed towards Poopy, screaming at the top of her voice, 'Run, Poopy baba, run!'

The dog turned and went straight for them. Poopy was nearest, and before she could jump aside he had leapt into the air and made a snatch at her bare arm. His teeth drew a thin line of blood, and the ayah's shrieks mounted to frenzy. Yusuf released me and rushed forward, but before he had taken more than a few steps he stopped, for Mr Delacourt was at the gate with a gun in his hand. There were two shots, and Buffer, after a convulsive movement, lay dead in the dust at our feet.

Round the still form everything was excitement. Mr Delacourt was holding Poopy's arm. My mother and father, attracted by the sound of the shots, had rushed downstairs, and my father dispersed the gaping crowd which had gathered. My mother led Poopy and Mr Delacourt upstairs. The De Souzas went reluctantly on their way, but Marise and I, in spite of threats and appeals, followed resolutely in the wake of Poopy.

Matters moved swiftly. The nearest Pasteur Institute in those days was at Shillong, and to Shillong Poopy must go without delay for anti-rabies treatment. The Assam mail train left at four o'clock in the afternoon and she was to be on it.

The question of who was to take her, however, presented serious difficulties. Mrs Delacourt, on hearing of the affair, had collapsed, whether from grief for her dog or her daughter nobody knew. Mr Delacourt had some vital business on his hands but was prepared to leave it and take Poopy away. There was an appeal in his eye, however, and my mother answered it. She would, she said, take Poopy to Shillong. I looked at her. Yes, I was to go too.

At this point Marise turned and ran rapidly downstairs.

Ten minutes later Mr Andros, pale and anxious, appeared among us. 'There has been trouble,' he said. 'I'm sorry I couldn't have been here to help, but I didn't know...'

'Don't worry, Mr Andros,' my mother said. 'Nobody could have done anything. Poopy'll be all right. We're leaving for Shillong this

49

afternoon.'

'Yes. It's very, very kind of you,' said Mr Andros warmly. 'But the children—they won't be too much for you?'

My mother smiled. 'No, of course they won't.'

'You are very kind,' said Mr Andros again. 'Is it necessary that Marise should take any warm clothing?'

There was a prolonged pause.

We all looked at Mr Andros, and presently he raised his eyebrows. 'It will be cold there, I think,' he said hesitatingly. 'If I may advise, you should take warm clothes for the children for the evenings. My wife is packing some for Marise. And if it is of help,' he continued, 'perhaps I may send one of my clerks to make the reservations. You will want to engage a first-class compartment that will have four berths, and I shall tell the man to see that there is a servants' compartment attached.'

My mother made a sudden movement and Mr Andros put up a detaining hand. 'No, please do not worry about fares now,' he begged. 'Leave it all to me, and when you have gone your husband and I will settle what each of us owes. And one more thing before I leave you, for you are busy. You will not need to take your ayah, for your other daughters will want her. Mrs Delacourt will also need an ayah while she is indisposed. If Marise's ayah could go with you, I beg you to use her as your own.'

Mr Andros went away to superintend his daughter's packing, and my mother looked at my father. 'Well?' she asked.

'Very awkward,' said my father. 'Very awkward indeed. But you can manage three. After all, you've managed three all these years.'

'But that child went back deliberately and...'

'Perhaps,' I put in, 'she thought you meant she had to go.'

'Yes,' said Poopy, 'I think she thought that.'

'It isn't a bad idea,' said Mr Delacourt. 'Marise'll be company for that one'—he jerked his head towards me—'while that one'—he indicated Poopy—'is having her treatment at the Institute.'

We left from Sealdah station that afternoon and had a very good send-off. Queenie and Cuckoo appeared, followed by Benny, who carried two jars of Mrs de Souza's homemade guava jelly and a large chunk of her famous guava cheese. They were put into our compartment, together with three large dolls, twelve tins of chocolate, three numbers of *Chatterbox*, an enormous volume called *Chums*, and a large assortment of comic papers—all gifts to Poopy from sympathetic friends.

She clambered into the compartment, picked up *Chums*, and took it out to Benny. 'Here—you'd better have this,' she said. 'It's all things for boys to read.'

Benny took it and gazed at it ecstatically. 'I can have it—for nothing?' he exclaimed.

'Yes,' said Poopy. 'I don't like boys' stories.'

'Well, all right. I'll have it,' said Benny. 'Good-by. You know what they'll do to you? They'll stick in needles. They give you twenty-eight injections, getting stronger and stronger, and that part takes about fourteen days, but it's better than getting hydrophobia, I'm telling you. I know a chap who told me about another chap who…'

At this point a whistle blew and Benny's cheering information came to an end. Before us was an eight-hour journey to Santahar, where we would change trains and travel through the night to Amingoan; at Amingoan we would board a ferry and cross the Bhramaputra to Pandu. From Pandu we would make a six-hour journey by car to Shillong.

We were met at Shillong by Colonel Melyard, at whose house we were to stay. He was an old friend of my father and had retired from active service some years earlier and settled in Shillong.

Colonel Melyard gave himself up completely to our entertainment. He took us for daily drives, sometimes round Shillong, sometimes far out into the Khasi Hills. We picnicked near and far. He took us to see ceremonial dances and reeled off as many facts about the local tribes as Benny himself could

52

have done.

Our last trip, when Poopy's inoculations had come to an end, was a picnic to Cherapungi. The outing was not a success. The rain came down steadily, collecting in pools on the curved brim of my mother's hat and overflowing in drips down the back of her neck. My own topee was a pulpy mass, and even Marise's elegant beribboned cover looked a sorry sight. Colonel Melyard appeared to be enjoying a joke all by himself and finally allowed us to share it. Cherapungi, he informed us, throwing back his head and roaring with laughter, was the world's wettest spot, with a rainfall averaging over four hundred inches a year. We tried to be impressed. My mother stuffed a large handkerchief into the back of her blouse and said, 'Oh, really!' Poopy took off her shoes and emptied some of the four hundred inches out of them.

We were sorry to leave Shillong and the white-whiskered Colonel. Back in Calcutta, we saw everywhere signs of the approaching cold weather. Round the lights flew myriads of tiny green flies. They fell in our food and followed us in clouds. There were cold early-morning mists and it was hot only in the middle of the day. We could return from our morning walks with our pinafores as crisp and fresh as when we set out. We went less often to the swimming baths and spent our time roller skating in the rink under the huge tent on the Maidan.

Early in December Marise left to stay with her grandparents at Chandernagore. We sat on the floor of her room and watched her ayah packing. We felt a little uneasy, for departure seemed to be in the air. My father was to go on leave in March and our passages were booked; we were to go down to Colombo by train and board an Orient Line steamer. Poopy was to go with her father and mother a fortnight later; they were going by a mail steamer from Bombay. We listened with less attention than usual to Marise's description of the Christmas festivities to be held in her grandfather's big house, and Poopy spoke thoughtfully. 'Can't you ask your father, Marise, to bring you to England? Then we'd all be there and we could see each other.'

'My father wouldn't go to England,' pointed out Marise. 'He'd go to Greece.'

'Well, your stepmother then. Couldn't she take you?'

'No, I asked her,' said Marise, 'but it's no use, because she doesn't come from England. She comes from Australia, and she's going in April to see her mother. She said she'd take me, but I don't want to go to Australia.'

'But if you asked your father...'

'I did ask him,' said Marise, 'and he said that if I ask my grandfather he'll take me with him to France, because that's where his home is. If I went to France,' she went on, 'you could come and stay with me. I've got lots of cousins and we could all stay together.'

France, we decided, was a better proposition than Greece or Australia and afforded some chance of meeting. It was arranged that Marise should persuade Mr Legrand to take her to France with him, and we waved her off with restored cheerfulness.

Poopy and I missed her, but we had a great deal to do. Buying presents for nine De Souzas was in itself a big undertaking. Besides this we had to make arrangements for the party we were to give for them. It was to take place at my house, and after a great deal of persuasion my mother had consented to let us have a khoi bag.

Khoi is puffed rice, and a khoi bag was an enormous bag made of the thinnest paper and filled with khoi. Into the middle of this were put innumerable presents of a lightweight variety, and the bag was suspended from the rod of the ceiling fan in the middle of the room. At the end of the party, the host or hostess climbed on a chair, assembled the guests in an expectant ring below the fan, and poked the bag with a long stick until it burst. Down tumbled the toys, and the guests, throwing themselves on the heap, scrambled for the presents raining down upon them. It was a sport peculiarly fitted to take a place on the spacious bare floors of an Eastern house and is not recommended elsewhere.

Our party went very well. Mr and Mrs Knox

had expressed a wish to be present. They sat at one end of the table and the De Souza family was ranged round the board with my mother, my two sisters, Poopy, and myself separating its members. My sisters began by being a shade aloof, but they warmed up remarkably during a game of 'Good morning, Brother Jonathan' and screamed louder than anyone during a game of hide-and-seek through all the rooms of the house.

It grew late, but it was obvious that the De Souzas felt that a good party could not go on too long. At last my father brought in a long pole and I was instructed to break the khoi bag. I gave a hearty prod, and the next moment the bag's contents were falling in a shower to the floor.

The rest of the evening was confused. The four De Souza boys, with a wild whoop, flung themselves on the floor, gathering all the presents they could seize. This was legitimate, but Chum and Nikko, introducing new rules, snatched the prizes which Poopy had collected. Before we knew what was happening, Queenie and Cuckoo, still on the floor, advanced on all fours towards the culprits and a battle royal began. The gentle Milly stood at the ringside, clasping her hands and appealing to the combatants to desist. Tutu made ineffective snatches at the windmill of arms and legs. The other six De Souzas were a tangled, heaving mass among the khoi. My father, Mr Knox, and Yusuf eventually separated the combatants, and when the khoi had been shaken from everybody's clothes, it was found that Queenie had lost several tufts of hair, Cuckoo's nose was bleeding, Benny's collar had been torn off, and Chum and Nikko had large lumps on their foreheads. My sisters had retreated early, and Poopy had crawled safely out of the scrum.

'What—oh, what will your mother say?' moaned my mother.

Queenie glared balefully at the causes of the riot. 'They cheated,' she said. 'When I tell my mother they cheated...'

'We didn't cheat,' shouted Benny. 'We didn't! It was a game, I'm telling you.' He walked up to my father and appealed to him. 'We had to snatch everything, isn't it?' he demanded. 'We didn't cheat—we were only snatching, like you said.'

With great tact and with a judicious distribution of the toys to the visitors, my father succeeded in restoring calm. The battered guests departed, clattering down the stairs with many expressions of thanks.

My father took out a handkerchief and wiped his forehead. 'Well, there they go,' he said. 'When's the next party?'

'If it's being held here,' said Mr Knox, 'I hope you'll remember to include me. I haven't seen a scrum like that since my rugger days.' He turned to me. 'Remember now,' he said. 'I'm to

57

come to all the parties.'

There were no more parties for some time, however, for on the night of Christmas Eve, Poopy was taken to the hospital with enteric. A few days later Benny followed, and we were left to watch with acute anxiety the progress of the two patients.

As the days went by my father brought me news, and soon I learned that Poopy was out of danger.

'And Benny?'

My father hesitated, and a dreadful fear filled my heart.

'And Benny?'

'They don't know,' said my father slowly, 'about Benny.'

CHAPTER SEVEN

They didn't know for some time about Benny. For a while his life hung in the balance and we could do nothing but wait and hope.

I was amazed, through all my anxiety, at the concern shown by the most unlikely sympathizers for his progress. My father's distress I understood; he had sat many an hour in the veranda, listening to Benny's lectures and thanking him courteously at their conclusion. My mother missed his visits and the long, steady, inquisitive brown stare, but I was unprepared for the frequency with which Mr and Mrs Knox came upstairs to ask for news. Mr Delacourt wore a frown of anxiety which was not caused by Poopy's condition. Mr Andros went daily to the hospital with fruit, books, and large woolly animals which I knew Benny would consider too juvenile, if he ever came to consider them. Mr Clavering and Charles Rogers, despite their former jibes at the De Souzas, called each evening to ask how the 'little feller' was getting on.

At Number Four, Mrs de Souza still worked each day with the dirzees. In the evening, firmly refusing Mr Delacourt's offer to take her in the carriage, she sent for a gharrie and, with Milly and Tutu, drove to the hospital, crept down the long ward, and looked at the unconscious figure lying behind the red screen. Then they drove home again.

We waited. I prayed and the De Souzas lit candles, but Kariman shook her head. How, she asked, brushing my hair for the night, how could that little Benny conquer disease? To pray was good, but it was a strong fever and he had had it long—too long. How much strength was there in that thin little body? How much...

'Oh, shut *up*,' roared both my sisters together.

Kariman's jeremiad sank to a low mutter, and I crept into bed and saw a dreadful picture of Benny's flower-decked coffin on its way to the cemetery.

When I woke the next morning, my father was standing at the foot of my bed. There was an odd expression on his face, but it was difficult to see clearly through the mosquito netting. I pulled it up, scrambled under it, and, seeing his face clearly, gave a yell that brought both my sisters upright in their beds.

'He's all right,' I shouted. 'He's all right, isn't he? He's better, isn't he? Isn't he?'

I threw myself on him, my arms round his neck, my legs curled round his waist.

'Whoa,' he grunted. 'Slowly does it.'

'He's better, isn't he?'

'He isn't better yet,' said my father, 'but he's turned the corner. His mother and Mr Delacourt were with him until four o'clock this morning, waiting. Then he took the right bend, and he's going to be all right in time.'

It was a wonderful morning. I wrote a piece of poetry which I look at still. It reads:

> We laughed, with Benny with us still,
> Then he got ill.
> We prayed, and Benny took the bend,
> He's on the mend.

Below, in my father's handwriting, is a note:

> Well, if that's verse,
> I've read worse.

I was not allowed to see Benny for some

time, but on the following day Mr Delacourt took me to see Poopy. We drove to the hospital and I followed him into the lift and out again, along wide corridors and past innumerable doors.

Poopy had a private room at the end of a corridor, and as we came near it Mr Delacourt halted and put a hand on my arm. 'One minute,' he said. 'There's something I must tell you before you go in.'

I waited.

Mr Delacourt seemed to have some difficulty in going on. 'Before you see Poopy,' he said, 'you must realize—well, she's been pretty ill, you know.'

'Yes. She'll be white, won't she?'

'Yes, she'll be pale—and thin, of course. But you see, when a person's very ill they sometimes have to—to—well, to cut their hair off.'

'You mean she's bald?'

'She—well, we'll go in, shall we? I wanted to warn you before you saw her.'

He opened the door. 'I've brought someone to see you,' he said.

'Hello,' said Poopy. 'I'm bald.'

I walked up to the bed and inspected her with frank interest. My eyes opened wide, for she had undergone a complete metamorphosis. Her head was encased in a natty little white cap; her face had altered in shape and was thin and small; her eyes seemed to have grown

61

larger. She showed none of her father's concern over her appearance.

'Do I look funny?' she inquired without anxiety.

'Are you quite bald?' I inquired.

'Well, there's something coming there,' said Poopy. 'You can feel it—it's soft and fluffy. Shall I take off my cap and show you?'

'No,' I said. 'Will it grow again soon?'

'Yes, of course,' said Mr Delacourt. 'It'll grow again in no time. You wait. Next time you see Poopy, she'll have sweeping tresses.'

No sweeping tresses appeared. But when Poopy came out of the hospital, nobody would have recognized her except for the fact that her clothes still met with the same unaccountable accidents, still hung lopsidedly, still required frequent pinning. She was thin and tall and her head was covered with a mass of fair, tiny curls. I thought her enchanting.

My sisters admitted that she was good-looking but added the usual criticism. 'Oh yes, she's *pretty;* but when they gave her some new hair, why didn't they give her some new expressions? She looks the same all the time— like this.' They pulled their faces into masks of complete blankness.

'But if you *look*,' I said, 'she *has* got lots of expression. If you know her, you can see it. Ask Marise. She doesn't say it just because I do, but because it's true. There's lots of expression in her face—lots!'

There was, but I knew that the casual observer would never see it.

The sight of Poopy had prepared me for changes in Benny, but when my father took me to visit him some weeks later he looked very little changed from the old Benny. He was a good deal thinner and his eyes looked larger, but his face, instead of looking pale like Poopy's, looked darker than ever. We found him propped up in his bed at the end of the ward, giving all within hearing a lecture on comets. Two of his audience had fallen asleep; the rest were regarding him attentively.

He broke off to greet us. 'You've come to see me?' he exclaimed in delight. 'So many people have come—my mother and Milly and Queenie and Cuckoo and all of them. And Chum and Nikko came at the wrong time and they didn't get in to see me. All the way home they went.'

'Do you think you ought to talk such a lot?' asked my father gently. 'You'll get rather tired.'

'Tired—with talking?' asked Benny in astonishment. 'There's only talking here. You can't walk about on the floor and you can't reach the other chaps' beds to play games. All day read, read, read—so sick of it I get, I tell you. These chaps don't know anything about comets; they haven't learned. But that chap over there, the small chap, goes to my school and he saw Halley's comet. You saw it?' he asked me.

I was doubtful. I remembered being wakened and taken on to the narrow back veranda of our old house; I remembered the darkness and the excitement. I remembered Kariman holding a coat round me and pointing upwards and my father explaining the rarity of the event. But I couldn't remember the comet.

Benny saw my hesitation and settled himself against his pillows. 'I will tell you,' he said.

'Well, I'll leave you for a little while,' said my father hastily, 'and come back presently.'

While Benny lectured I looked around at his fellow patients, all of them smaller or larger editions of Benny: thin, dark, with relations and friends clustering round their beds. The ward seemed to be full of fruit. Nurses were busy labeling and carrying out tray loads of apples and oranges, guavas, peaches, and pomalos.

I realized that Benny had finished his lecture and was asking a question. 'When,' he inquired, 'will Marise come?'

'Marise? She's still at Chandernagore, but if you're here when she comes back she'll come and see you. She'll have to come back for school soon.'

'You-all,' said Benny, 'are going to England soon, isn't it?'

'Not soon—March.'

'And Poopy—they're going also?'

'Yes.'

'You'll come back?' There was no anxiety in the question. Benny merely wanted to know. I said that I could only speak for my own family and not for Poopy, but we certainly would come back.

I was sure we would. There had been a half-hearted suggestion from my father about leaving my mother at home with us, but he had received no support. My sisters and I knew little of England. I remembered nothing of our last visit and heard nothing in my sisters' imperfect recollections that could stir up any enthusiasm for a return visit. England was home—but there was no need to stay at home.

Mr and Mrs Knox were to go home on the same ship as Poopy, and Mrs Knox was looking forward to bringing out her sister, who had never seen the East.

When Marise returned from Chandernagore, Mr Delacourt, anxious to give Poopy a change before her return to school, decided to take the three of us on a week's trip up the Sunderbands, the creeks and waterways which make up the delta of the Ganges. Poopy had long been promised a trip on one of the little paddle steamers that went up and down the river, and Mr Delacourt thought that she would be happier with us for company.

It was a wonderful trip. There was little, outwardly, to account for our enjoyment on a tiny boat with strictly limited deck space, nosing slowly in and out of narrow waterways. But we had the steamer to ourselves and at night our searchlight pierced the thick jungle and turned it into a fairyland. Mr Delacourt retired to a chair in a corner of the deck and we were left to ourselves, without Kariman, without Rosie, without any ayah.

Each morning the mess steward, a tall, imperturbable Goanese, presented himself before us with a grave bow. 'Will you order the meals, Missies?'

Certainly we would. We would have fruit and ham and eggs for breakfast, served on deck. We would eat lunch in the little saloon—soup, fish served in those shells, please, with mayonnaise on top. And prawn curry—no, not prawn, because it upsets Poopy—vegetable curry, please, with those tiny little new potatoes and cauliflower.

'Yes, Missies. And pudding? Ice cream—strawberry, vanilla?'

'Oh yes, thank you, lovely. And tea on deck, with those little fancy biscuits, and dinner on deck—no, not on deck because all those insects fly about at night and bang into our faces. Dinner inside—soup and fish and then—well, anything you like, and ice cream—can we have ice cream twice?'

'Certainly, Missies.'

Mr Delacourt had a tiny cabin on one side of the steamer; ours, equally small, were on the other side. The deck space was limited, but it was enough for us. We spent the long cool days lying on a rug on the deck, reading or chattering. The steamer nosed into an inlet, tied up at a tiny landing place, untied again, and backed away.

There was no time to do the round trip and we came back by train. My father was waiting for us at the station when we reached Calcutta, but instead of the tall figure of Mr Andros, Marise's grandfather stood on the platform looking, with his elegant hat and neat beard, exactly like the pictures in our French books.

Marise saw him as the train stopped and gave a cry of delight. 'You see?' she said triumphantly. 'He's come!'

'Who's come?' asked Poopy.

'My grandfather. Don't you remember? I was going to ask him about going to France.'

We looked at her eagerly. 'Is he going to take you? How do you know?'

'When I asked him,' said Marise, 'he said he didn't know yet. But he'd see. Then if everything was all right, he was going to come and ask my father and settle everything. And now he's here.'

'Well, go and ask him if it's all right,' said Poopy.

Marise grasped her grandfather's arm eagerly as soon as she reached his side and broke into a torrent of French. We waited patiently for a translation of Mr Legrand's reply and sighed with satisfaction. Marise was to go to France. We should not be too far apart after all.

When we reached the house, I ran eagerly upstairs to my mother. She embraced me, I thought, a little absently, and her eyes were fixed on my father with an anxious look.

'I am worried about Eileen Knox,' said my mother. 'She was taken to the hospital an hour ago—the same trouble.'

We all looked sober. Three times Mrs Knox had been taken suddenly and inexplicably ill with mysterious symptoms; her face swelled and became hideously bloated; her lips looked thick and pendulous and her temperature rose alarmingly. I had caught a glimpse of her as she had left the house the last time, and had lain awake half the night in horrid remembrance. The doctors were unable to trace the cause of her attacks, but it was agreed that it was a form of poisoning.

The afternoon wore on, but my mother's absent-mindedness seemed to increase. My father was out but returned at about five o'clock and addressed her several times without getting a reply. She handed him a cup of tea from a tray which Yusuf had brought in.

My father looked at her curiously. 'Dreaming?'

My mother roused herself. 'No—not dreaming,' she said. 'I'm just thinking.'

'Children, pay attention,' directed my father.

'Don't joke. I'm thinking about Eileen.'

'Well, what about her?'

My mother spoke hesitatingly. 'It's probably very silly, but I've got an idea in my head and I can't get it out again. I keep remembering that each time she's been seized by these awful attacks it's been on the day she marked her linen. Don't laugh at me.'

'I'm not laughing,' said my father, 'but I don't see very much connection.'

'No, I don't either. But I can't put it out of my head. The first time, you remember, she sent for me and I found her down there looking dreadful. I got her off to hospital, but I remember seeing a pile of linen laid out beside her on a table. She had marked it that morning. And the next time and the next—sometimes sheets and pillowcases, once some new shirts she'd had made for her husband. Would that be just coincidence?'

'Well, it sounds like it. What would marking linen have to do with a virulent attack of poisoning? You've marked our things scores of times.'

'Yes.' My mother looked dejected. 'Couldn't marking ink poison anybody?'

'Well, if they drank a couple of bottles I've no doubt they'd feel . . .'

'But Eileen,' said my mother, 'doesn't use that sort of ink.'

'No?' There was a change in my father's

voice. 'No? Well, what does she use?'

'She makes it herself,' said my mother. 'She noticed that the markings made with ordinary marking ink always faded, but the marks the laundryman put on himself stayed quite clear and lasted until the garment wore out. Eileen asked him what he used, and he brought her a—well, it looked like a kind of nut, and he told her to boil it and use the liquid. She showed me the nut and said she'd ask for one for me, but I didn't want the bother of getting hold of a saucepan and going into the cookhouse and—and generally messing about. Eileen prepared the stuff in one of the bathrooms, over a spirit lamp. Then she poured the liquid into a saucer and did her marking. It was wonderful stuff for lasting, but I'm certain—I can't tell why it is—but I'm certain that there's some connection between that and—and her illness.'

There was silence for a time. The situation was serious, for each of Mrs Knox's attacks had been more dangerous than the previous one, and it was becoming vital to discover the cause.

My father came out of a reverie and spoke. 'I think we'll go into this,' he said. 'Don't mention the matter to anyone else just yet, but it wouldn't do any harm to get hold of this laundry fellow and ask him a few questions. Is he the same as ours?'

'No, but the servants would be sure to know where he lives.'

'Probably. But if we send for him and fire off a lot of questions,' said my father, 'he'll get frightened and lie like a trooper. When's their laundry day?'

Nobody knew. Yusuf, summoned, said that it was every Friday. Friday was too far away.

'Do you know where he lives?' asked my father.

'Yes, Sahib.'

'Well, send somebody to find him,' said my father. 'Tell him that we'd like him to bring along whatever it was he gave the Knox Memsahib to make names on her washing.'

Yusuf looked at my mother with his calm brown eyes. 'There is plenty of marking ink still,' he informed her. 'If you wish...'

'No, Yusuf. This is very special marking dye. Send a messenger and tell him to bring the laundryman and the thing for marking ink. Tell him we'll pay him.'

At half past seven that evening Yusuf entered the drawing room. Behind him waited Mrs Knox's laundryman. Yusuf was told to bring him in, and the man came and stood, salaaming and expectant, before my parents.

My mother put out a hand and the man placed in it a small brown nutlike object. 'That, Huzoor,' he said respectfully, 'is what you asked me to bring.'

My mother looked at it. 'Is this,' she asked, 'the same as the one you gave the downstairs Mem-sahib?'

'Yes, Huzoor.'

'And I have to put this into a saucepan and boil it?'

'Yes, Huzoor. You boil it for a time. Then you take out the liquid which it makes.'

There was a pause. My mother, with a disappointed little shrug, turned to my father and dropped the nut into his hand. 'Well, there it is. It doesn't look harmful, does it? Perhaps I've been silly. Pay the man and...'

My father looked thoughtfully at the nut. 'This thing,' he said to the man slowly. 'You use it yourself?'

'Yes, Sahib, always. It is very good.'

'I see.'

'All the laundries,' proceeded the man, 'use it, and then the clothes do not get lost.'

'I see,' said my father once more. 'But in England we like to make sure, before using these things, that they are—that they cannot harm the children if they are left about. This is quite ... harmless?'

The man smiled and spread his hands wide. 'Of course, Sahib. I have used it for twenty years, and my father before me.'

There was another pause. There seemed nothing more to say. My father handed the man some money, and with a deep salaam he turned to go.

Passing my sisters and myself, he gave another salaam and as he did so, a thought seemed to strike him. He turned. 'There is only

72

one thing, Sahib, about the little Miss-Sahibs.'

'Well?'

'Do not let them go near the saucepan when it is cooking.'

My mother's eyes, wide and eager, stared at him. 'Why?' she asked.

'Because the liquid itself, *that* is not harmful, Huzoor,' said the man, 'but when it is cooking, the fumes—ah! They are very bad. Do not let the children breathe them.'

He was through the doorway before my mother was able to speak. She called after him, her voice schooled to calmness. 'If the children breathe the fumes,' she asked, 'what then?'

'Ah, Mem-sahib,' said the man, 'that would be bad.' He shook his head from side to side. 'Very, very bad,' he repeated. 'Their faces would become swollen and they would be very ill. You must keep them away.'

Yusuf followed him out and we were left staring at one another. My father's eyes fell to the thing he held in his hand. 'Well, you were right,' he said. 'We'd better get hold of Knox.'

My mother had indeed been right. Mrs Knox had breathed the poison as she bent over the preparation. Her cure was a simple matter. A repetition of the attacks was impossible, and nothing could exceed Mr Knox's gratitude. My mother emerged from obscurity to become the neighborhood's most-talked-of woman. I told the story to Mrs de Souza on the following morning and saw her mouth opening as she listened.

'Oh my!' she exclaimed as soon as I had finished. 'You didn't know? If you had asked *me*, but! If you had said what she was doing, I would have said "Go, go, tell her how dangerous!" That's the bhellia nut. My, she might have been poisoned!'

Here, a few houses away, was somebody who could have warned us all of the danger. My opinion of Mrs de Souza became higher than ever.

CHAPTER EIGHT

The arrangements for Marise's visit to France were completed by this time. Marise's stepmother was to visit her own relations in Australia. She and Marise would travel down to Madras together, and there Marise would board a Messagerie Maritime liner to be met at Marseilles by the Legrand cousins.

The time sped on until only a few weeks remained before our own departure. We would be followed closely by the Delacourts and Marise. With departure imminent, we began to feel a little cooler about leaving.

Our house looked very empty. Our books, linen, china, glass, and crockery were stored in packing cases. Trunks were packed with our personal belongings, or those belongings considered by my father to be necessary for our journey. We were, he ordained, to travel light and traveling light, we discovered in tearful indignation, meant discarding wholesale such treasures as doll's houses, large Teddy bears, miniature cooking stoves, jack-in-the-boxes, and innumerable objects, the accumulation of years. Would my father, I inquired incredulously, would he have me go to England and leave Susie behind? Susie was my biggest doll, half life-size, with a pram so large that Poopy and Marise had frequent rides in it. Susie, said my father, was not traveling. Susie could stay here in a packing case or Susie could be given away.

And Dorothea?

Dorothea, too.

And Bessie? And Louise?

Those also, and their beds with the striped mattresses and the patchwork quilts. It was regrettable but we could not, said my father, make our way to England weighed down with a dozen trunks full of toys.

Kariman, appalled by the decree, developed an uncanny gift for slipping treasures into unsuspected corners of trunks. My father showed as uncanny an instinct for finding them. After the first shock our philosophical natures reasserted themselves. We took the toys to the hospitals and won an unmerited reputation for generosity.

There was a large crowd at Howrah station

to see us off. Mrs Andros and Marise, the Delacourts, Mr and Mrs Knox, and the entire personnel of the chummery—these formed the inner circle of the throng. Next came less intimate friends and, on the fringe of the throng, our servants. Kariman forced a way to the compartment and gave us a good deal of parting advice. Yusuf made up the four berths in our compartment and my father's, next door. The chummery sang songs of farewell and Queenie, Cuckoo, and Benny arrived with an assortment of jars that made my mother turn pale. She took them and added them to the mountainous pile on the floor of the compartment. We were to be in the train for five days; we had provisions for five weeks.

Throughout the hubbub I stood at the carriage door, close to Poopy and Marise.

'You can write from Colombo,' said Poopy. 'After that we won't be here, so you'll have to send the letters to Skye.'

'Write to me a lot,' said Marise, 'and I'll write lots, too.'

'And don't forget to say what boat you're coming back on,' said Poopy.

I put an anxious question. 'You won't let your mother leave you behind at school, will you, Poopy?'

'No. I've told you and *told* you. I'm coming back.'

Whistles blew. The train gave its siren signal. The servants gave a final salaam. As the train

76

began to move, Benny, with a flying leap, jumped onto the step and was yanked off by an indignant official.

I saw Poopy and Marise waving their arms, and raised my voice above the din. 'See you in November!'

The voyage was smooth as far as Port Said and very rough thereafter. We carried our tropical clothes down to the baggage room and reappeared with heavy, unfamiliar coats and suits and struggled into them. The warm, friendly decks became cold, wet surfaces where a few hardy souls lay in deck chairs, swathed in rugs. The Suez Canal was no longer a geographical feature. It was the line between this cold sun and the blazing one we had left behind. My sisters and I, united in adversity, watched bewhiskered gentlemen go for a couple of turns round the deck and return to shelter, rubbing benumbed hands and blowing pinched noses.

'B'Jove, little girls, it's good to feel this air again, isn't it? Body in it, body in it! Puts life into you, bucks you up, whips up your blood and makes you feel alive. B'Jove, it's fine!'

We were very glad to see them enjoying it. For ourselves, we preferred unwhipped blood.

We found England interesting. On Sundays everybody put on their best clothes and behaved very quietly. English clothes, even on Sundays, were made of wool and tweed in very dull colors. English shoes were sensible but heavy, like the English schoolgirls we met. English food was less varied than Indian food, but there were larger helpings and one was expected to eat them. English servants were distant and unapproachable; one could not go into the kitchen and sift the lentils or grind the chilis for the curry—even if there was curry. English schools expected pupils to attend every day and wanted to know why they didn't if they didn't.

The English, on their side, took stock of us. They had heard all about children from India—spoiled, arrogant chits, given to lording it over an army of cringing bearers. We were scarcely lordly types, but we were patently untrained. Fourteen, and didn't know how to cook an egg! Thirteen, and had never cleaned a shoe! Ten, and thought that every bedroom had a bathroom of its own!

We adjusted ourselves to the new conditions. The English accustomed themselves to us, and on both sides the feeling remained that it would not be for long. In October, in November at the latest, we would go back to a land where it rained only when one expected it to, where bathrooms abounded, where one wore the lightest, the palest, the prettiest of filmy frocks. The months would soon go by. A little patience, and then...

The months went by and August came. August, 1914.

Before August ended, my father had sailed

for special duties in Mesopotamia. His cousin Frances had given her house to the Red Cross and had come to live with us. The lease of our house was renewed indefinitely. My sisters and I accepted the new conditions without fuss, even without comment. There was a war, and we were here until it ended. We looked at one another and there was no need for words.

We were trapped.

CHAPTER NINE

We went back to India in 1920. I was sixteen and a half, my sisters nineteen and twenty. My mother had died during the war, and Cousin Frances had been a guardian with whom we were on the most friendly terms until the Great War ended, when we began a private war of our own.

I was the storm center. My father, who had spent the war years in Mesopotamia, was now back in India and had taken a flat, installed our long-stored furniture, and sent for us. Cousin Frances thought it right that my sisters should go but said that I should remain and continue my musical training. I raised a loud cry of protest and my sisters, greatly to my relief, came in strongly on my side. I needed support, for Cousin Frances had a case. I was showing more than usual promise and was to study under a series of eminent teachers. Was I, demanded Cousin Frances with a fierceness we had never suspected in her, was I to throw away all this and go back to a mere Gumm?

I said that I was; my sister agreed with me. My father remained neutral, and we began to fear that Cousin Frances would carry the day. But I began to lose weight, and the letter which my sisters wrote to my father would have terrified the most stolid parent. My father cabled by return. We were to sail in October. 'All of us,' said the more jubilant of my sisters, burying her head in a cushion lest Cousin Frances should hear her triumph. 'All of us! One, two, three of us.'

We arrived in Bombay at the end of October. My father met us and we traveled across India together. We thought him completely unchanged, but he spent the journey looking at us in bewilderment.

'Which is which?' he inquired. 'Where's the skinny little one with the plaits?'

'Where,' we inquired, 'are we going to live? Are we still in Minto Lane?'

'Minto Lane? No, not there,' said my father. 'It's running to seed a bit. I've got a flat in Russell Street—remember Russell Street? It's a lower flat unfortunately, but I couldn't get an upper one at a price to suit me. I think you'll like it.'

'Running water?' inquired the more practical of my sisters.

'It's all in order,' said my father. 'Nice wide veranda with a marble floor, looking out on a tennis court. Big bedroom for the two of you and a smaller one for the little 'un, and nice tiled bathrooms in a chessboard design.'

'And Yusuf and Ali—will they be with us?'

'Yes, and the old cook, too. You won't recognize Ali. He's a very smart young man now.'

We thought Calcutta very much changed, though my father said that it was just the same. The gharrie had been superseded by the car. Noisy taxis, driven by Sikhs with one hand on the wheel and the other on the horn, scuttled up and down Chowringhee. There also seemed to be a great many more young men. We had barely arrived when some of them became aware that at least two girls had been added to the city's meager total. One or two of the bolder spirits remembered a slight acquaintance with my father, and soon our drawing room was over-run by young men with fair hair or dark hair, with small moustaches or without, with blue eyes or brown. I had nothing to do but try to sort them out, for it appeared that nineteen and twenty were more alluring ages than sixteen. I learned names, but before I could fit them to their owners' faces a new set had appeared. Peons with smart uniforms waited daily on our steps with letters. I took them, signed in the little book, and delivered them to my sisters. In due course I brought out a reply or intimated that there wouldn't be one. I played tennis with a confusing series of athletic young men in beautiful flannels and a sun tan.

And through it all I thought about Poopy and Marise.

My correspondence with Marise had lasted until war began. Her last letter had mentioned the prospect of a visit to a countess in France, and on this high note our correspondence had ended. Poopy had written fairly regularly. At the outbreak of war Mrs Delacourt had fled to America. Poopy's last letter had been written on her way home across the Atlantic. Her mother had died two months earlier and Poopy hoped to come back to India before very long.

I made inquiries about Mr Andros, and my father said that he was still in Calcutta and was reputed to be a rich man. Where he lived or what Marise was doing nobody seemed to know.

'I know someone who'd be able to tell you,' said my father. 'Mrs Knox.'

'Is she still in Minto Lane?'

'Yes. She was in England throughout the war like you, but she came out just after the armistice. Her husband kept the Minto Lane flat and they're in it now. It's time you girls went along to see them. They've always asked me how you were getting on, but whenever I try to get hold of your sisters they seem to be surrounded by this crowd of whoever-they-are.

Tell me,' he asked. 'Am I losing my mind or do we keep getting a fresh lot? I get used to a face or two and then they disappear and a fresh lot arrive. I suppose your sisters know what they're doing?'

'Oh yes.'

'I'm not so sure. How is it that young what's-his-name was dancing round with one of your sisters one week and the other the next? Did he change his mind?'

'No, they changed theirs. Sometimes they change over when they get tired of someone.'

'Good heavens! Two months ago,' said my father wistfully, 'I was leading what was practically a bachelor existence, and now I'm in a monkey house. What about you? Don't you like monkeys?'

'I don't know. Not much.'

'And another thing—what about your music?' asked my father. 'Hadn't we better make some sort of arrangement to have you go on studying with Miss Gumm?'

'Where is she?'

'Same place,' said my father. 'She used to play for one or two concerts for war charities, but they tell me that once she got at the piano nobody could get her away again.'

I giggled. 'Yes, I know.'

'Well, go along some time and look up Mrs Knox,' said my father. 'She'll be glad to see you.'

I walked one evening to Park Street and

paused for a moment at the corner of Minto Lane to glance up at the flat in Minto Lodge where Poopy had lived. I remembered the pretty, foolish Mrs Delacourt and wondered what had become of the ayah with the little stool. On earth or elsewhere I was certain she was still sitting on it. I went slowly up Minto Lane and found a slight feeling of excitement rising in me. I felt uncertain of myself, as though with each step the years were falling away and leaving me as I used to be in this lane—thin, ten, and topee-clad.

Number One—was it still a chummery? It looked like it. There was an evening jacket airing in an upper window and a pair of trousers dangling from another. There was the same row of fern pots flanking the entrance, the same shade of bilious green lining the veranda screens.

Number Two! The upper story was occupied; I could see servants moving here and there. With an odd feeling of confusion sweeping over me, I stared for a few moments at the familiar windows, and was roused by seeing a servant coming towards me.

'Knox Mem-sahib?'

She was in. The man led me through the dark entrance hall, through the swing doors into the drawing room. I stood hesitating while the servant went in search of Mrs Knox, and in a few moments saw her coming towards me with outstretched hands.

'Oh, my dear, I *am* glad to see you!' She took my hands and held them while her eyes went over me. 'Well, well, well, well, well! Pink cheeks and no more matchstick legs! How good it is to see you!'

She led me to a chair and we settled ourselves for a chat. She was tall, though not so tall as I remembered, and her hair was grey. In other ways she seemed the same. She was stiff and upright, still unapproachable and forbidding to the eye. For the first time I noticed how beautifully she spoke.

'I want *all* your news,' she said. 'But first, what will you drink? Barley and lime? So will I.' She ordered the drinks and prepared to listen to as much family news as I could give her. She spoke affectionately of my mother and smiled when I told her of the struggle there had been to keep me in England. She made no comment, and I put a question. 'Do you think I was wrong?'

Mrs Knox laughed, and I found myself liking her more and more. 'Of course I think so,' she said. 'But you must leave me to quarrel with your father about it. What about your old friends?' she asked. 'I suppose you've been writing to them?'

'Well, no, not lately. But my father says that Mr Delacourt and Mr Andros are in Calcutta.'

'You're a little out of date with your Mr Delacourt,' said Mrs Knox. 'He's Sir Guy now. He's been Sir Guy for a year or two and he's a very important person. Did you know his wife was dead?'

I nodded.

'Poor Poopy!' Mrs Knox leaned back in her chair and laughed. 'Do you remember her safety pins?'

'Yes. Do you ever see Mr—I mean, Sir Guy? Do you know whether Poopy's coming out again?'

Mrs Knox looked at me in surprise. 'Coming out? Why, didn't you know?' she asked. 'She's not only coming out—she's on her way out.'

'You mean she's—she's . . .'

'She's on the same ship as my sister,' said Mrs Knox. 'She's on her way now. I met Sir Guy at a dinner party,' went on Mrs Knox, 'and he asked whether my sister would consider bringing Poopy out with her and keeping an eye on her on board. They'll be here in a fortnight. The twenty-first at Bombay, so I suppose that means the twenty-third here. Are you glad?'

I was very glad. I was more glad than I could explain.

'Do you,' I asked, 'know anything about Marise?'

'Marise? Oh—Marise! That's the other one, isn't it? The third of the trio!' Mrs Knox shook her head. 'No, I'm afraid I don't. Her father's here, of course.'

'Is he still living at Number Three?'

86

'Oh, no, no, no!' said Mrs Knox. 'Nobody of any note—except ourselves, of course!—lives in Minto Lane any more. I think he lives at his club, but I can't really tell you. Marise—I remember her now—what a little miss she was, with her bracelets and her silks and laces! Dear me, how it takes me back! I remember that dreadful ayah of Poopy's, trailing behind with the little cane stool, and Marise's ayah—she was the grand one, wasn't she? And yours was the fat one who was always scuttling after you, holding out your topee and telling you to put it on. What became of her?'

I told her, thankfully, that we had not set eyes on Kariman since we left her at Howrah station years ago.

It was time for me to go. I walked slowly out of the gate and, pausing, looked to the left down the rutted lane to the corner round which I had turned so many times in the past, bound for Number Four. I had not asked Mrs Knox about the De Souzas; I had thought once or twice of questioning her about them, but the news of Poopy's return had decided me. It had been Poopy, in the past, who had come with me on that first visit to the De Souzas, and I would wait until she came so that we could go together if she wanted to go. I found myself staring at the dusty road, my mind starting at the top of the scale and running down unhesitatingly.

Milly
Tutu
Queenie
Cuckoo
Pijjy
Benny
Chum and Nikko.

The lane seemed full of them, and they seemed to be beside me on the way home, taking me back to my ten-year-old self so completely that when I passed the fat figure squatting at the entrance to our flat, it merged into the picture and became part of the whole. Only when it began to perform strange antics of welcome did I realize with horror that this was no dream—it was the all-too-solid flesh. It was Kariman!

With a yell of surprise, I bounded up the steps, rushed through the hall, and confronted my sisters. 'K-Kariman! She's here! She's there! She's outside!'

'Don't we *know*?' said the more stricken of my sisters. 'Can't we *hear*? She came just after you went out. We saw her; we said, "Hello, good-by." She said, "I've come back," and we said, "Oh no, you haven't." Then we conducted her out firmly, and there she's been ever since, going on like that. Listen to it!'

'From the time you were born,' chanted Kariman from below, 'each one of you I nursed in my arms. In health, in sickness, I nursed you, I dressed you, I fed you, I washed

88

you, I put on your clothes, I undressed you, I put you to bed, shielded you from danger. I watched over you, I...'

'You see? It's been going on for hours. It'll go on, unless we have her carried out of the gate by four coolies, all day and night.'

'Well, *let* her go on,' I said. 'It's all right for you two—you got rid of her ages ago, but I was the one who had her last. Didn't you tell her we're miles past the ayah stage now?'

'We told her everything—several times. I told her and she told her and Yusuf told her and Ali told her and then the rest of the servants told her, one by one. And now listen to her. Everybody'll think we've ill-treated her or done her out of some money or something. Heaps of people are coming to play tennis and they'll hear all about the way she undressed us and put us to bed. She's already told the whole neighborhood about how I bit her when I was four. She made it sound as though we'd never had our teeth out of her. Well, *let* her. Let her howl the house down.'

For some days the unwanted applicant returned early each morning, took up her position on the steps, and left—hoarse but hopeful—each night. On the fifth morning, to our incredulous, thankful wonder she was not there. With our hearts light and gay, we finished our breakfast and saw my father off to his office, his face, too, showing pleasure and relief. But when he returned that evening, lines of care were newly etched on his brow. Kariman had merely moved her pitch; she had spent the day on the office steps, giving out in a monotonous wail the history of her long association with my mother. My father moved his papers to a room at the back of the building. Kariman followed him round and seated herself, rocking to and fro, beneath his window. My father stood it as long as he could, but when Kariman, her voice rising to high C, informed him that he was her father and her mother and that the bones of his dead wife were rattling in sorrow for her beloved ayah, my father's nerve failed. He came home and joined with us in our lamentations, and a week later Kariman, a look of ineffable smugness on her face, began her new duties.

She no longer spoke in Hindustani. She persisted in talking to us and to the maddened servants in a particularly hideous semblance of English. She had, on the strength of my mother's carefully worded letter of recommendation, obtained a post with a woman who had no children and had acted as lady's maid.

'I not ayah now,' she informed us. 'I laydissmaid. When you go that time to Balight, I work as laydissmaid. I sew, I iron, I mend. When you have little baby, I will be ayah. But now I am laydissmaid.'

The laydissmaid installed herself, going about her duties with a low, contented purr.

90

She did not now follow me about, but as she was constantly in view, ironing in my bedroom, washing in my bathroom, folding and tidying, it was difficult to believe that I was really free from her guardianship. I worried little, however. My mind was fixed on Poopy's imminent arrival.

On the night of the twenty-third my sisters dined out. My father dined at home with me and then went to his club to play bridge. Yusuf carried out my coffee to the veranda and I sat on a comfortable chair in the semidarkness, dreaming. The mail train would be in; Poopy was at this moment in Calcutta. Soon, perhaps even as soon as tomorrow, I would see her. I wondered whether I ought to ring her up first or wait until she had settled down. I wondered what she would be like and whether we should be friends; whether her hair was still curly, her face still expressionless.

A car drew up and stopped in the porch. I looked at my watch and wondered what had brought my father home so early and why he did not come up the steps and into the drawing room. I craned my neck round the back of my chair and peered back into the lighted room. Yusuf was coming towards me, and behind him was something blue—a dress, a slim form, a...

'Poopy!'

Forgetful of my precarious posture, I craned forward, and the wicker chair, toppling,

91

deposited me on the marble floor. I scrambled up and Yusuf righted the chair, looking with a new interest at the newcomer as he did so.

'Oh, Poopy!'

Her face was as pretty as ever—and her expression as blank. Her voice was as flat and as unemotional as it was when she said good-by, six years ago.

'Hello,' she said.

CHAPTER TEN

Poopy and I met every day and talked all day. My sisters admitted that she had grown very pretty; that her hair, a mass of soft, fair curls, was unusual and effective, that her figure was good; but they regretted that the years had not taught her how to use her face muscles or keep her clothes in order. Pleats still came out, shoulder straps fell down, suspenders snapped. Before I had said two sentences to Poopy I was offering her a safety pin.

We had a lot to talk about. I gathered that her education was where we had left it. Poopy had been to more American schools than the Americans, but she had left again before there had been time to assimilate any knowledge. She talked of prairies and deserts, ranches and mountains, cañons and beaches, but she had no idea where any of them were. She heard of my years of steady progress without envy and was glad that I was not to be a famous pianist.

Dismissing the past, we looked into the future and wondered whether it would bring Marise.

Poopy's news of her was later than my own. 'She wrote about once or twice a year,' she said, 'but her letters got more and more French. Sometimes there'd be whole sentences I couldn't make head or tail of. But she stayed with the countess. Did she tell you that?'

'No, she was coming to it. Did she say anything about...'

'Marble staircases? The place was full of them,' said Poopy. 'The countess liked her, and I don't wonder, if she looks anything like the snap she sent—the same curls and a very French frock.'

'If we could get hold of Mr Andros, Poopy, we'd find out where Marise is, wouldn't we? Couldn't we go to his office or ring him up or something?'

We decided that this was the best thing to do, but on the following evening something happened which made the plan unnecessary.

I was to play at a charity concert, and we gave a dinner party before it. We asked Mr and Mrs Knox, Poopy's father, and a selection of my sisters' young men. I was to play in the first half of the programme, and during the interval I went round to the front of the theatre to join our party. I saw Poopy in the foyer, coming towards me with a long, cool drink in each hand.

'This is ginger beer,' she said, 'and this one's lemonade. Which?'

'This one, thanks,' I said. 'How did I play?'

'It sounded all right,' said Poopy cautiously.

I took a sip of my drink, raised my head, and saw coming towards us the tall, handsome figure of Mr Andros.

He came up to us and looked at us quizzically, his head on one side. 'I seem to remember,' he said, 'these two young ladies.'

'Oh, Mr Andros,' I said breathlessly, 'we were going to ring you up or come and see you or something. We...'

'And I,' said Mr Andros, 'was coming to see you. But I saw your name on the programme tonight and came out here to look for you.'

'Where's Marise, Mr Andros?' asked Poopy, who liked to come straight to the point.

'Marise is—let me see,' said Mr Andros slowly, his face screwed up in calculation. 'She'd be about latitude—now what? I'd say about latitude...'

'Is she on her way out?' asked Poopy.

'Say latitude thirty degrees, longitude—well, say twenty-five degrees,' said Mr Andros, still frowning. 'Or say just crossing the Tropic of Cancer.'

'When does she arrive?' asked Poopy.

'It is better,' said Mr Andros, 'to allow for the tides and for the storms, too. If a storm...'

94

'Stop teasing and tell us,' I begged. 'Poopy's going to spill her ginger beer in a minute.'

Mr Andros laughed. 'She will arrive on Wednesday. She is coming by train from Bombay,' he said. 'She asked me if you were both in India, but I couldn't tell her because I didn't know. She will be glad,' he added.

'We'll come and see her,' I said. 'Where are you living?'

He told us. The address conveyed nothing to me, but Poopy told me some facts about it when we went back to our seats. 'It's huge,' she said. 'They'll be able to lend it to the Governor when Government House gets burnt down.'

'Wednesday—that's five more days,' I said. 'It won't be long.'

There was a lot to do before Wednesday. I had to go and see Miss Gumm and ask if she would teach me again. My father and I walked one evening to her house and were led by a servant into the garden, where Miss Gumm stood in the center of a small lawn upon which were laid four or five beautiful tiger and leopard skins. Two small boys were lifting up one of the skins and shaking it, under Miss Gumm's supervision. She saw us and, stepping through the rugs with surprising agility, took my hands and worked them up and down like a pump handle. This done, she looked so anxious to return to the rugs that my father hastened to state our business. Miss Gumm listened and, before he had said three words, was shaking her head slowly and lugubriously from side to side. Undeterred, my father went bravely to the end of his request, only to learn that Miss Gumm would not be in Calcutta very much longer. Her doctor had recommended a cold winter to tone up her blood. Miss Gumm had taken part of a house in Darjeeling and was to leave her present quarters in less than a month.

She waved a hand at the outspread rugs. 'Already, you see,' she said, 'I am bagging.'

We stood looking at one another, a little dismayed. I was keenly disappointed. I felt that though Miss Gumm's method might be peculiar, I would be able to work far less well with anybody else. There was nothing to be done, however. My father made his farewells and said that it was a pity. I thought it a great pity, and Miss Gumm went even further.

'It is a grade, grade biddy,' she said, standing among her treasures and looking after us sorrowfully.

We went home feeling a little low, and I spent so long sitting on my bed regretting Miss Gumm that I forgot the time and was recalled by seeing my sisters almost ready. We were all to dine with Mr and Mrs Knox, to meet her sister. I got hurriedly into my long dress, glad for once of the ministrations of a laydissmaid.

Mrs Knox's sister was called Miss Brooke. She was plump, placid, and quiet. While others chattered, she bent quietly over a piece of embroidery, looking up now and then to put in a word. Her eyes were brown and humorous, and she had a way of giving an unexpected gurgling little laugh when anything amused her. We all liked her, and it would have been a pleasant evening if it had not been for the obvious illness of Mr Knox. He had not been well for some time, and my father, looking at his drawn face and frightening pallor, begged him to send us all home and invite us another evening. Mr Knox, however, protested earnestly. More than anything he enjoyed the society of old friends, and he had not seen my sisters since they had returned to India.

The evening wore on, and I knew that my father was uneasy. We left early and we had barely got into our own flat when the telephone bell rang.

'I'll go,' said my father.

We stood round him, vaguely apprehensive, and knew by his expression that something was seriously wrong.

'Who is it?'

'Mr Knox. You girls get to bed,' said my father. 'I'm going back.'

'Is he—is he ill?'

'He's collapsed. The doctor's there. Get into bed and get off to sleep, all of you,' he directed. 'There's nothing you can do.'

The telephone bell rang as we were getting into bed. My father said that he would not come back that night. Mr Knox's condition was grave.

In the morning we awoke to find my father in the house. He had had a bath and a shave and was waiting for Yusuf to bring him some breakfast.

'I'm going back,' he said, 'and I'll send Miss Brooke back here while I make all the arrangements with Mrs Knox.'

'Arrangements!' I stared at him. 'Arrangements? You mean he's...'

'He died at three o'clock this morning,' said my father. 'He'll be buried at three this afternoon.'

We paled. Last night Mr Knox had dined; tonight he would be lying under a few feet of earth in the cemetery on Lower Circular Road.

'How is Mrs Knox?' I asked presently.

'She's all right. She's known for some time that his health wasn't all it should be, but she hoped that the change—they were going to the hills in the hot weather—would pull him up a bit. She's got herself well in hand, but if you girls will look after Miss Brooke today and try to cheer her up a bit, you'll be doing something useful.'

We looked after Miss Brooke until the time came to put her in the car in which she would follow the coffin. After the funeral my father brought Mrs Knox back with him and she stayed with us for two nights. Then she and Miss Brooke went back to Minto Lane and began the task of clearing up Mr Knox's

98

affairs. Mrs Knox would have liked to settle her affairs and leave immediately for England, but her sister had barely set foot in the country and she felt it selfish to take her away immediately. Another difficulty was the lease of a house in the hills. Mr and Mrs Knox had taken a fairly large house in Darjeeling for the season and had paid a substantial deposit.

Before anybody could see a way out, Poopy made a suggestion. 'Why,' she asked me, 'don't you go to Darjeeling and stay with Mrs Knox and Miss Brooke?'

'Me?' I was staggered. 'What on earth for?'

'Well, for two things,' said Poopy. 'If you were in Darjeeling, then your wonderful Miss Gumm that you're so keen on could give you music lessons. That's one thing. And the other thing is that you'd stay with Mrs Knox as a paying guest, and that'd help her with the rent of the house. And if you and I both paid, then...'

'You?'

'Well, why not me?' asked Poopy reasonably. 'If I told my father that you were going to Darjeeling and if he knew that it would be a help to Mrs Knox, he'd grab at the chance. He's been trying to find some way of repaying her for letting me come out with Miss Brooke. He thinks they're both marvellous. Go on. Ask your father and see what he says.'

I put this proposition before my father, and his opinion of Poopy rose greatly. 'That girl's got a headpiece,' he said. 'Yes, it's a sound idea. I'll put it to Mrs Knox.'

He put it to Mrs Knox, who put it to Miss Brooke. The plan was adopted, the matter arranged. Poopy and I were to go with them to Darjeeling at the beginning of March.

This being settled, we had nothing to do but wait for the arrival of Marise.

Marise arrived on Wednesday. On Thursday she telephoned to me. On Friday I arranged that my father and my sisters should lunch elsewhere, and invited Poopy and Marise.

Poopy arrived just after breakfast and we spent the morning in speculation. I could tell her nothing of the telephone call except that it had been brief and that Marise had appeared to have a slightly French accent.

'We'll soon put that right,' said Poopy. 'Did she bring in the countess?'

'No, but when I asked if she'd like me to send for her, I'm sure she said she'd come in 'my' car. Does that mean she's got one of her own?'

'I wouldn't be surprised,' said Poopy. 'Her father always adored her—next to the tigers. She probably has a laydissmaid, too.' Poopy gave a sigh. 'I'm glad she's coming,' she said. 'It didn't seem the same without her, did it?'

'No. I bet she'll be pretty, don't you?'

'Yes, and smart. My father says she'll be as smart as paint. What time's she coming?'

'Well, I said one o'clock lunch and asked her to come early.'

At a quarter to one we walked slowly out and stood on the steps of the entrance. We were restless and a little uneasy. We had no way of knowing how we should be feeling by the end of this meeting. I turned to say something to Poopy, and at the moment we heard the sound of a car.

'That'll be . . .'

I stopped. There was a crash as something scraped against one of the sides of the gateway. An open two-seater, cream-colored, bumped into sight, flattened a bed of cannas by the entrance, and made straight for the gardener, who was bending over a rose bed. With a yell of terror, he leapt for the wall and hung there, clinging, as the car passed him. It knocked over a small tub of ferns and came to a grinding stop at the porch.

There was a brief silence. A liveried chauffeur sprang from the dickey, threw an anguished glance at the car's mudguards, and opened the door for his mistress. Marise stepped out.

For a few moments we merely stood and stared at each other frankly and, to my surprise, without embarrassment. When it came to the point, curiosity had overcome all other emotions. We wanted to see, and so we stood there and looked. Poopy and I saw standing before us the same finished product we had first set eyes on six years earlier. The curls were subdued, but the lovely little face,

101

the self-possessed air, the beautiful clothes—these were the same.

Marise turned to the chauffeur and issued an order, and he answered respectfully.

'Why,' asked Poopy, as we settled ourselves in the veranda, 'does he call you Shann Miss Sahib?'

Marise removed a small white hat, smoothed a white linen dress, and smiled charmingly. 'Jeanne,' she said. 'You see, out here they always called me Marise, but my name is really Jeanne-Marise with a hyphen. In France it was always Jeanne-Marise, which is, of course, more correct.'

'I see. Well, you'll have to excuse us,' said Poopy. 'We've been Marising you for so many years that it's sort of stuck now. Did you like France?'

Marise, it appeared, had liked France very much. The countess, of course, was genuine. Marise had gone to school with her two daughters, but she had not stayed long and her education, like Poopy's, seemed to have died at a very early age.

We made polite inquiries about her grandfather.

'I saw him in Paris,' said Marise, 'only two months ago. He looks old, but then...' She gave a shrug. 'And my grandmother is dead.'

'The one you used to go and see at Chandernagore?' asked Poopy.

'Yes, she died.'

'Oh, I'm sorry,' I said. 'But she was always a bit delicate, wasn't she?'

'She was old,' said Marise. Her next remark was on a very different topic. 'Do you go out with lots of men?' she inquired.

Poopy gazed at her in surprise. 'Men? Well, sometimes,' she said. 'My father gives parties, and people ask me to go to dances and things, but I'm not keen.'

'But'—Marise looked puzzled—'isn't anybody in love with you?'

'Heaps, I should say,' said Poopy, 'but they keep it to themselves. They go away and die quietly in corners and don't bother me with it.'

Marise's gaze passed to me. 'And you?'

I searched feverishly through files and found nothing.

'She's a bit young,' said Poopy. 'I suppose wherever you go they all fall flat on their faces?'

'You can joke,' said Marise, 'but in France a lot of men wanted to marry me. I could have been married again and again.'

'No, you couldn't,' said Poopy. 'Catholics can't marry again and again. And Marise, don't keep shrugging your shoulders in that French way.'

'French way? Can I help it,' asked Marise indignantly, 'if I have French ways? Can I help it if I talk in French? For years I was in France.'

'For years,' said Poopy, 'I was in America. Do I begin every sentence with "I reckon" and "I guess"?'

103

Yusuf announced lunch and we went into the dining room.

'Do you remember Mrs Knox?' I asked. Marise drew herself poker-straight and assumed a severe expression and I nodded. 'Yes, that one. Well, her husband's just died.'

'Poor thing,' said Marise.

'Her sister's out here on a visit, and they've got a house in Darjeeling for the season. Poopy and I are going to live with them.'

'Live with them where?' asked Marise.

'In Darjeeling. Miss Gumm—my music teacher, if you remember her—is up there, too, so I'll be able to go on with my lessons.'

'How long,' asked Marise, 'will you go for? Just for the hot weather?'

'No. They took the house from March to October.'

'March to October?' Marise put down her knife and fork and looked from me to Poopy in dismay. 'March to October! You mean you're going away—both of you—from March to October?'

'Yes.'

There was a pause. Marise was thinking and we did not interrupt her. 'But there's nothing,' she said dismally, 'to do up there! March to October—with nothing to do!'

'The town band plays at the Town Hall on Thursdays,' said Poopy. 'And if that isn't enough for you, you can join the club and play tennis and dance.'

'Dance? Who is there to dance with?' demanded Marise. 'A few government people, mostly old; a few tea planters, mostly away at their tea gardens; a few sick men coming up from hospital to get better!'

It sounded unpromising, but neither Poopy nor I could offer any consolation.

'Why,' said Marise, 'can't we only go for the hot weather and come back here when the monsoon begins?'

'We?' repeated Poopy inquiringly.

'Of course, we,' said Marise angrily. 'March to October! Do you think I can stay down here all by myself while you two go up there for all that time? There'll be nothing—nothing to do. We shall look at each other day after day, and that will be all.'

'Practically all,' admitted Poopy, 'but it'll be cool anyway. If you're coming, you'll have to ask Mrs Knox first. I don't suppose she'll mind. She'll be rather pleased, in fact, because it'll mean more money.'

'Money? What money?'

'Your money,' said Poopy. 'You're going to be a paying guest.'

'Paying guest? You mean I've got to pay something?'

'Something quite substantial. My father saw to that when he fixed the terms,' said Poopy. 'What did you imagine, that you were going to live on somebody from March to October for nothing?'

'But if I asked you to stay with me,' pointed out Marise, 'you wouldn't have to pay anything.'

'Certainly I wouldn't. You'd have to pay me,' said Poopy. 'What'll your father say if you leave him and go off all that time?'

'What do I say to him,' asked Marise, 'when he goes to tigers? He goes. *Alors*, I go.'

'*Alors*, you'd better ask Mrs Knox,' said Poopy. 'We more or less told her you'd be coming, but we waited to see what you were like first.'

'And what,' asked Marise, 'am I like? You're just the same—both of you. One is blunt and the other is polite. Do you see,' she went on, 'that we are all exactly the same size now? You and I, Poopy, used to be taller.'

We measured ourselves after lunch and found we were very much the same everywhere.

Marise ran her eyes down Poopy's dress and tweaked it into shape, muttering shocked protests. 'What happens to your clothes?' she asked. 'Look! Pull that down, like that. And this line goes along *there*, Poopy, can't you see?'

'It went along *there* this morning,' said Poopy, with as little resentment as Marise had shown at her remarks about the French gestures.

'I buy good material and I wear well-cut dresses and I put them on the right way round.

106

What more can I do?'

'You can see that they stay the right way round,' said Marise, pushing in a straying shoulder strap. 'You don't take enough trouble.'

A few days later the three of us climbed into Marise's little car and headed for Park Street. We were going to call on some old friends.

We left the car in Park Street and walked slowly down Minto Lane. We passed Number Two and stopped to stare at Number Three.

'Look how dirty it's got,' said Marise. 'And look at the compound, nothing but those ferns and cannas.'

'That's all there ever was,' said Poopy. 'And perhaps it's dirtier or perhaps it looks the same, only we notice it more now.'

We approached the gate of Number Four and turned into it. If Number Three was shabby, Number Four was ramshackle. We walked forward slowly, taking in the details as we went, each of us silent and absorbed.

An untidy servant came out and Poopy spoke to him. 'Does the De Souza Mem-sahib live here?'

The servant repeated the name slowly and then shook his head. 'De Souza Mem-sahib? No, Miss-Sahib.'

It was a shock. We were here at last on De Souza territory, back in spirit with the companions of our youth. The man's words roused us with an unpleasant suddenness.

For a few moments we stood irresolute and then seemed to realize there was nothing to wait for. With a glance at a dark young woman who had just appeared on the veranda above us, we turned and walked slowly to the gate. We were scarcely through the wide gateway when from behind came a sudden, piercing shriek.

It was a dreadful sound. Marise started violently and clutched my arm. Together we swung round and looked to see where the scream had come from.

It came again and two more, even shriller than the first, followed from the upper veranda. The dark young lady was leaning precariously over the shaky railing, waving both her arms in frenzy and screaming incoherent phrases. 'Come, come! Don't go, don't go. Come, I'm telling you! Wait! Wait for me. I'll come! Wait! I'm coming!'

We thought for a dreadful moment that she was coming over the veranda. She recovered her balance, waved her arms, rushed into the room behind, reappeared, waved her arms, and screamed again. She seemed to be anxious to come downstairs and terrified that before she got down we should have vanished. Her scamperings were exhausting to watch, but something about the movements was beginning to stir our memories—something familiar—something...

The cry came from the three of us

simultaneously. 'Tutu!'

The word had a magical effect. Tutu came to a dead stop halfway between the room and the veranda and, after a second's pause, crept on tiptoe to the railing and peered down at us. 'You know me?'

'Tutu!'

Tutu's face became irradiated. 'I'm coming,' she shrieked, and vanished.

We met halfway up the stairs. Tutu held Poopy's hands. A step lower, Marise and I were leaning over the banisters and clutching the hands of Queenie and Cuckoo, who had appeared from a downstairs room. At the head of the stairs Mrs de Souza, garbed in a flowered dress, held both arms above her head in an access of welcome and joy. We all talked at once, loudly and excitedly, but our three voices were unheard amid the nasal outcries of the family.

We got upstairs and in time found ourselves seated in the drawing room. We gave some account of ourselves and managed to slip in some questions in between. When at last we took breath, we had caught up with the De Souza news.

The servant had not, we found, misled us. The mistress of the house was no longer Mrs de Souza, for two years ago she had married Mr d'Almeida. She had given up the dressmaking business to Queenie and Cuckoo, who now sat daily in the workroom downstairs. Milly was out at the bazaar, but she would be back for dinner.

And the boys? All, said Mrs d'Almeida with pride, all in jobs. Pijjy had passed his examination with great credit and now had a class of small boys at his old school. Chum and Nikko—we'd never guess, said Mrs d'Almeida, and we didn't. Chum and Nikko were at sea—only apprentices now, but they would rise.

'Where,' I inquired, 'is Benny?'

Benny, we learned, was in Darjeeling. He was working in a photographer's. In a few months he would try to get into a firm of photographers in Calcutta.

When at last we rose reluctantly, the De Souzas came downstairs with us and saw us off, standing at the gate and waving until we were round the corner.

'Do you still like them?' Poopy asked me.

'Yes. Do you?'

'Yes. But it's like being at a play. I don't feel I'm part of it any more. Move over, Marise, and let me drive. I've practiced twice at home in our car. Go on, move over.'

Marise moved over. I got in and sat beside her.

'Which thing is it?' asked Poopy. 'I push this one, don't I?'

'No, that one.'

Poopy pushed it. I clutched the door and the chauffeur crouched in the dickey. We were off.

CHAPTER ELEVEN

We left for Darjeeling early in March and our departure was quiet. Only Poopy's father, Marise's, and mine, and my sisters stood on the platform beside our carriages. We had three berths in one compartment and Mrs Knox and her sister shared a coupé next door.

I parted from my sisters reproachfully, for they had seen and availed themselves of an opportunity to get rid of Kariman. They had suggested to Mrs Knox, with the appearance of great unselfishness, that the ayah would be of use in waiting on Poopy, Marise, and myself in Darjeeling, and the suggestion had met with Mrs Knox's approval. No protests from the three most concerned had been listened to. Kariman was an old and trusted servant and she would relieve Mrs Knox of the necessity of employing a stranger in Darjeeling.

Besides Kariman we were to take Mrs Knox's cook and both her bearers. They stood a little self-consciously by their bundles of luggage, the latter swollen by the addition of new warm clothing.

When we had waved until the little group on the station platform could be seen no more, we turned to inspect the fourth occupant of our carriage. The name on the card pinned to the carriage door had read 'Mrs Vrishna.' A few minutes before our departure a white-bearded servant had assisted an Indian lady into the carriage, arranged her luggage, and left, herding three younger servants towards the third-class carriages farther down the train.

We inspected Mrs Vrishna discreetly. She looked young and was short and solidly built. She said nothing, busying herself with unpacking, but she glanced at us once or twice. Something in the glance or the eyes or the hair disturbed something deep in my memory. Once disturbed, it kept stirring. It stirred at intervals throughout the first hour of our journey and then I startled everybody by giving a triumphant shout.

'You're Cloma! Cloma—I can't remember your other name, but you *are* Cloma, aren't you? I *knew* you were. Poopy, don't you remember? She was in my class at the Convent and then they put her in a higher one because she went on so fast. Isn't that so, Cloma? I didn't recognize you at once because you've got so...'

I pulled myself up before the word *fat* actually burst out, but Cloma supplied it with a gentle smile. 'So fat,' she said. 'It's terrible. I can't think where it'll stop.'

Her English was perfect, her voice—in Poopy's words—smooth and creamy. She wore a sari of the palest pink, its edges beautifully embroidered with silver thread. It was not of a color or texture well adapted to traveling on a long and dusty journey, but there was not a speck or a crease in it, and Cloma herself seemed as unruffled as her attire.

The name, she said, was changed. She was now married. She had been married for three years. She paused considerately to let this piece of information sink in. She was younger than two thirds of her absorbed audience. She had a house in Darjeeling but she had been to Calcutta to visit her father and her husband for a short time.

Our tongues went faster than the train, and we were all taken by surprise when we found that the station into which we were now drawing was the dinner stop. The train carried no restaurant car, and the passengers descended and made their way into the large station restaurant while the train waited. Neither Mrs Knox nor her sister, we found, wanted any dinner. They were not good travelers and preferred to stay in their carriage or walk up and down the platform. We sent them a tray of tea and biscuits and settled ourselves with Cloma at a table for four.

When we left Cloma and went to say good night to Mrs Knox before the train went on again, we learned a shattering piece of news. Mrs Vrishna, said Mrs Knox, had been to Calcutta to visit her husband and her father, who were political prisoners. They were in jail. Worse still, Poopy's father had practically put them there.

113

I thought that Poopy was actually going to register emotion, but the moment passed and her face remained blank.

She was silent for so long, however, that Marise looked at her curiously. 'What are you worrying about?' she asked. '*You* didn't do it. And anyway she can't know about it. Look how nice she was!'

'Of course she knows about it,' said Poopy.

We climbed into the compartment. Cloma had spread her bedroll on her lower berth and was shaking up the pillows as we entered. 'Who,' she inquired gently as we came in, 'is the lady with Mrs Knox?'

'Her sister,' said Marise. 'Did you know Mr Knox had died?'

'Yes.'

'Well, the sister had only just come out to India and Mrs Knox had taken a house in Darjeeling and now we're all going to share it.'

'What,' asked Cloma, 'is the house called?'

'It's got a frightening name. It's called Landslide House,' I told her. 'Do you think that means it'll go down the hill with us all in it during the monsoon?'

Cloma smiled and shook her head. 'I think you're safe,' she said. 'It's built on rock, but they called it Landslide House because it was being built when they had that terrible landslide there, about 1899. Have you heard about it?'

We nodded.

Cloma continued a little dreamily. 'It was a bad one,' she said. 'My grandmother tells some dreadful stories; she was there. She watched her children running back to the house and she didn't know whether they would ever reach her or be buried on the way. Whole houses ... whole families! The hillside looked so permanent, she said, and then suddenly an enormous piece of it would just tear off and go down.'

'I say!' protested Poopy, and Cloma laughed.

'I'm sorry. Your house,' she went on, 'was built for a man who never lived in it.'

'I suppose he got torn off and went down?'

'I'm afraid so. So they called it Landslide House—unwisely, I think, because it isn't lived in enough. The name seems to frighten prospective tenants. The house,' she ended, 'is just above mine. We shall be neighbors. I hope you'll come and see me and meet my two sons.'

'Your two ... Y-you've got two sons?' said Marise in a choked voice.

Cloma nodded. Marise climbed up to the upper berth we had allotted to her and sat on it, gazing across with an awe-struck expression at the serene Cloma.

It was an uneventful night. Three of us put on nightgowns and slept dreamlessly. We left Cloma still in her pink sari, leaning against the pillows. In the morning, though her bed looked slept in, she was still sitting there, wide-awake, smiling, the delicate pink sari as fresh as ever.

At Siliguri we parted from her. The old servant entered, rolled up her bedding, and conducted her to the waiting Toy Train.

We gave our luggage to some coolies and knocked on the coupé next door to see how Mrs Knox and Miss Brooke were getting on. They had not enjoyed the night, but Tom Cheep looked very cheerful.

I had forgotten Tom Cheep. He was a canary, bought in Minto Lane by Miss Brooke from an Indian who was selling them. She had become extremely attached to the little thing and had insisted on bringing it with her. His cage was handed out and we promised to look after him. Would Mrs Knox come with us and have breakfast? No, thank you. They wanted only tea and toast and would join us in the Toy Train.

The mention of the Toy Train made Poopy look more expressionless than ever.

'What's the matter?' I asked.

'Toy Train,' she said. 'If they can't stand an ordinary train, how're they going to stand about six hours of joggle-joggle-joggle? And this Tom Cheep! Who ever heard of taking a bird up in the Toy Train and expecting it to get up alive? Haven't they ever heard how joggity it is?'

'Mrs Knox ought to know,' I said. 'She's been up before.'

'Well,' said Marise, 'if they don't know,

they'll find out in time.'

At the first sight of the little train with its small powerful engine, Miss Brooke exclaimed with delight. 'It's *sweet*. It's so *sweet!*' she said. 'It reminds me of the little funiculars in Switzerland. Look at those little carriages with open sides, Eileen. Why didn't you tell me about this sweet little train?'

'The Darjeeling Himalayan Railway,' began Mrs Knox in a dry tone, 'has a two-foot rail gauge and without benefit of racks or cogs rises from a three-hundred foot level here at Siliguri to over seven thousand feet at Ghoon in forty-five miles and drops again at...'

She stopped, and we knew why. There was no need to tell Miss Brooke of the hair-raising twists and turns we were to make, of the thousand-foot drops we should graze, of the towering mountains up whose slopes we should rise. Everything would be met as it came.

The first thing that came was nausea. The scenery, which became more and more wonderful, could make no impression on our two unhappy companions. The train stopped frequently, backed, shunted, climbed again, but the pauses were too brief to be beneficial. One by one the tiny stations were left behind: Sukna, Rungtong, Chunbati. At Tindaria, the fourth, Poopy made a sign, and Marise and I followed her to the platform.

'Come on,' she said. 'We'll look for another

117

carriage. They'll be much better by themselves.'

We told Mrs Knox of our intention and she looked grateful. We took our cases and walked up the platform. Suddenly Poopy, with a muttered exclamation, turned and went back to the carriage. She returned a moment later and we saw to our surprise that she was carrying the canary's cage.

'What on earth,' demanded Marise, 'do we want with that thing?'

'Look at it,' said Poopy, indicating the drooping, dejected Tom Cheep. 'If he lives till we get to Darjeeling, I'll eat his cage.'

'But...'

'Miss Brooke feels bad enough now,' said Poopy. 'If her bird dies under her nose, she'll probably throw herself out of the train with grief. She went pea-green when we did that last hairpin bend round that chasm.'

We found places in a carriage and settled ourselves. The air was cold, the view breathtaking. We put our coats on, leaned over the side where the view looked most dangerous, and would have been thoroughly happy if we could have forgotten the canary. But the jerky, swaying motion of the train, which we were enjoying so much, was obviously proving fatal to poor Tom Cheep. We did what we could. We held his cage firmly. We let it swing gently to the train's movement. We took him out and tried to make him warm and comfortable. It was no use. The engine fussed and puffed loudly. It blew off steam; it blew its shrill whistle; it took us onwards in neck-jarring jerks and stopped with rude abruptness.

Soon Poopy took a scarf and draped it reverently over the cage. 'In future,' she said, 'Tom Cheep will be known merely as Tom.'

We looked at her, startled.

'You mean...'

'He'll never cheep again,' said Poopy.

We were, on the whole, relieved; it had been a harrowing sight. We took out some fruit which we had bought at Siliguri and ate it, leaving aside for the time being all thoughts of Miss Brooke's feelings when the news should be told.

We were ready for a meal when we reached Kurseong and were glad to stretch our legs, but one glance at Mrs Knox and Miss Brooke convinced us that it was better to leave them alone for the present.

'I bet,' said Marise, 'when we get up to Darjeeling, Miss Brooke'll find she can't stand the height. Has she ever been over seven thousand feet before?'

'I don't suppose so,' said Poopy. 'She won't worry about that, though—not when she hears about the bird.'

We reached Darjeeling. The train, delighted with itself, gave a final shriek and scurried along the road, for during the last few minutes of the journey the tracks of the little railway actually ran along the cart road, passing close to the native shops and causing great inconvenience to pedestrians too deaf or too absorbed to hear the engine as it came round the frequent bends. Another corner or two and the station roof, looking like a row of greenhouses perched in the air, came into sight.

We had arrived. The air was cold and we longed to get into the sun outside the busy little station. Sturdy little Bhutia coolies picked up our luggage and hung it, heavy trunks and all, on straps passed round their heads. Rickshaw men crowded round us. We chose the smartest-looking rickshaw we could see and put Mrs Knox and her sister into it.

'Will you be all right?' asked Poopy. 'We'll see the luggage off and come along later.'

'Thank you,' said Mrs Knox. 'Somebody's going to meet us at the house with the keys.'

She looked better and Miss Brooke was beginning to turn from green to pink. With firm ground under her feet and the prospect of eating and sleeping in a house, she could almost smile again. She followed her sister into the rickshaw and looked at the covered cage of the late Tom Cheep.

'How is my little cheeper?' she asked.

'Don't you think about *him*,' said Poopy. 'The cook and the bearers have gone on ahead with Kariman. They'll be at the house before you, and you must make them get a nice meal for you at once. Then you'll feel better.'

We saw them go and Poopy looked broodingly at the cage she was carrying. 'I could lose it by mistake,' she said, 'or it could be stolen or something.'

'No, we'll tell her,' said Marise. 'Let her bear it like a—a man.'

'I want to walk. I'm stiff,' I said. 'How far is this Landslide House?'

We found Cloma and asked her. It was rather a long way, she said—a matter of two, two and a half miles along the cart road. We could get in a rickshaw and go along the lower road and then climb up by hill paths.

We left the station, dodged an impertinent little engine which raced round a corner and missed us by a hair, and walked slowly along, looking at the sights as we went. The sun warmed us. We passed little wayside shops full of grain, cloth, sweets, cakes. The smells were strong and varied and not always pleasant. I moved nearer to Poopy to avoid two little Bhutia babies tumbling in the road and felt her hand clutching my arm.

'Hey!' I said involuntarily. 'That hurt!'

Poopy ignored the complaint. 'Look!' she said.

We looked. She was pointing to a dirty little shop with a miscellaneous collection of wares.

'Look at what?' asked Marise. 'Rice, chilis, dusters, Indian cigarettes, matches?'

'Oh, don't be silly. Look *there!*'

We followed the pointing finger. Above the

121

shop hung a small wooden cage and in the cage was a little yellow bird. No further words were necessary. We stood still and waited while Poopy spoke to the man. 'How much?' she inquired.

The hillman's face, round and pleasant, broke into a smile. Ah, no, it was not for sale.

Poopy argued and pleaded. We joined her and added our voices, which must have become higher, for an interested crowd of little Bhutia boys gathered round us. We went on for some time and then gave it up. The man was adamant. There was no sale.

We walked on a few paces and I stopped. 'I say,' I said thoughtfully, 'couldn't we work it another way?'

'What other way?'

'Well, all these Bhutias are gamblers. All the rickshaw men gamble. Whenever they're waiting anywhere they always start that dice game, whatever it is. If we could offer to...'

We were back, standing before the man, grinning as widely as he.

'Listen,' said Poopy. 'We'll toss you. Heads we get the canary and tails you lose it.'

There was a roar of appreciation from the greatly enlarged crowd.

'Oh, no, no, no!' said the delighted shopkeeper.

'Very well! Heads we get the canary, tails you get six rupees.'

'Oh, no, no, no!'

'Well, heads we get the canary, tails we don't.'

It was done. The nearest Bhutia boy produced, astonishingly, a rupee and a jovial rickshaw man offered to do the tossing. The rupee went up; it came down. Heads. The crowd roared. The shopkeeper promptly leapt up and brought down the wooden cage.

'You may keep the cage. We don't want it,' Poopy told him.

She distributed some money to the most helpful of the watchers and we went on our way. The cover was off Tom Cheep's cage and a lively little canary was hopping about inside.

'There, that'll please her,' said Poopy, swinging the cage in careful triumph. 'She'll never know the difference. They're both yellow. I wish we could have given poor old Tom a decent burial. It seemed unkind to leave him in a drain.'

We walked on with brisk steps and took a road leading uphill. At the top I stopped, and it was my turn to say, 'Look!'

I had seen the snows before and so had Marise. To Poopy the sight was new and silencing. We gave her as long as we could and then Marise pulled her on.

'Come on, I'm hungry,' she said. 'Where's this Landslide House?'

We stopped a passing hillman and asked him. He pointed down a steep, narrow path and indicated that if we took it we should come to the house.

We walked down carefully, for the path dropped with dangerous steepness. It leveled out and we saw a signboard leaning at a drunken angle. We put our heads on one side and read the words, *Landslide House.*

'The board looks like it,' commented Poopy.

'Well, this is it. Come on.'

We pushed open a creaking wooden gate and gazed at the building before us. For some time we stared, unable to speak.

'Is this it?' asked Marise slowly, at last.

'Yes,' said Poopy. 'Can't you see?'

'Yes. It was kind of Cloma,' I said thoughtfully, 'not to tell us.'

CHAPTER TWELVE

Landslide house afforded us, while we were still young enough to profit by it, a perfect example of buying, or leasing, a pig in a poke. The agents, replying to an application made by Mr Knox from Calcutta, stated that the house contained a spacious combined drawing and dining room on the ground floor, with a glassed-in veranda, two bedrooms, and two bathrooms. The upper floor consisted of one extremely large bedroom, two dressing rooms, and two bathrooms. Off the upstairs bedroom, said the agent, was a second glassed-in veranda overlooking what he claimed to be the finest view in Darjeeling.

He was right in every particular. We agreed that we ourselves, in Mrs Knox's place, would have taken the house unhesitatingly. But certain details were omitted from his letter, and these we learned by disagreeable degrees when we took possession of the house.

Only from the side could the extraordinary position of the house be fully appreciated. It was, as Cloma had told us, built upon rock, the only drawback being that there was not nearly enough rock. Undeterred by this lack, the builders, running out of ground, had gone on building into the air. Half the upstairs bedroom, which we were to occupy, and the whole of the upstairs balcony jutted over the edge of the rock and hung over a seemingly bottomless chasm. We never discovered what kept the jutting-out part from breaking away. We might have inquired, but we thought it better not to know. There was the view, if we ever had the courage to stand on the balcony and look at it. The mountain panorama was straight ahead, wooded slopes to right and left, the abyss below. It would, said Marise, be like being up in a balloon. But none of us had ever felt the slightest desire to be up in a balloon.

The first evening was chaos. The cook, after inspecting the cookhouse, a tin-roofed erection about ten yards from the house, picked up his bundle and vanished without the formality of farewells. The bearers, after a glance at the servants' quarters, followed the cook. We joined Mrs Knox in indignant condemnation and wished very much that we could go too. We were cold and hungry and the interior of the house did nothing to raise our spirits. The furniture was poor, the rugs threadbare, and the walls full of cracks and holes through which someone could put a boot—and evidently had. There was electric light but only one bulb, which we had to screw on to whichever light we wanted to use. There was a great deal to do and nobody but ourselves to do it.

Kariman, after one horrified look around, had burst into tears and settled down in a tiny entrance hall to cry it out. Did we expect, she asked, that she would sleep out there in that cold, damp hut and catch her death? Was this the place to bring a laydissmaid who had worked only in the best service all her life? Where was warmth, where was food, where were the decencies?

Accompanied by this wailing, we worked. With numbed fingers we opened trunks, unrolled bedding, and got out what we needed for the night. We screwed the solitary bulb into first one socket and then another. On switching on a light in the bathrooms, we found that there was no water and no taps. A small zinc bathtub stood empty in each bathroom; an empty jar stood beside the tub.

126

In this crisis we decided to enlist Cloma's aid if we could find Cloma.

'She said the house was below ours,' said Marise.

'That might mean anything,' said Poopy. 'It might be under our rock, somewhere miles below that flying-buttress balcony of ours.'

'Well, it must have a gate,' said Marise. 'We'll walk down that side road and see what we can find.'

'We can't go without a lantern,' I pointed out. 'The road isn't lighted.'

We found a lantern in the woodshed. Leaving Mrs Knox and Miss Brooke to prepare a scratch meal, Poopy, Marise, and I took the lantern and made our way cautiously out of the side entrance.

The road was even steeper than we remembered. We stumbled down it, looking anxiously to the right. On the left there was nothing but the yawning valley over which our balcony hung. It seemed a long time before we came to an opening with a neat board which read, *Silver Lodge*.

'Do you think she lives here?' asked Marise.

'Well, somebody does,' said Poopy. 'Come on.'

We walked up the drive, our spirits rising as we approached the brightly lit house. Another light sprang up in the porch and we saw the bearded servant who had attended Cloma on the train.

'Mrs Vrishna?'

He bowed and we entered, following him into the drawing room. In another moment Cloma was before us and we were pouring our woeful tale into her ears.

'No water?' she said at the end. 'But there must be water. There's a sweeper permanently attached to the house. He acts as caretaker and he's always there.'

'Well, he isn't there now,' I said. 'Perhaps he followed the cook and the bearer and ...'

'No,' smiled Cloma. 'He's a hillman. Wait a moment and I'll see if our servants know anything about him.'

Her servants knew a good deal. The sweeper was ill. His brother had been sent for but lived a good many miles away over the hills. He was on his way and would arrive in the morning.

'And in the meantime,' said Cloma, 'I'll send our sweeper up and he must fill all your jars and heat some bath water for you.'

More than this, she insisted on sending us one of her bearers until we could obtain new servants. She also promised to send wires to Calcutta with news of our safe arrival. Mine read, 'Safe but servants fled. Please send up Ali.' Ali, I felt, would be someone to lean on. Once he arrived, everything would settle itself.

Cloma gave us a warm invitation to stay and have dinner, but we refused. We could not sit down to a good dinner and leave Mrs Knox and her sister to tinned salmon. Cloma then

128

filled three baskets with butter, bread, milk, hot-water bottles, firewood, and electric bulbs. With these we returned in greater state than we had come out. The servant went before us with his own lantern. We followed with ours and two small boys brought up the rear with the baskets. The borrowed bearer came last.

Dinner was a scratch affair, eaten as close to the fire as we could push the table. The butter was thick and yellow and we piled it on thick slices of bread and ate like wolves. Afterwards we went upstairs and pushed our three beds as far away from the balcony as we could get them. Each time we had to walk on the jutting-out side of the room we went step by step, like skaters testing the ice. Kariman refused point-blank to set foot beyond a point halfway across the bedroom, and we were secretly relieved. Her weight, we felt, would have been too much for the overhang. On the other hand, she had wailed and snuffled without ceasing since our arrival, and we should not have regretted seeing her fifteen stones vanishing through the floor boards. We decided to give her one of the dressing rooms, and the speed with which she stopped crying convinced us that this was what she had been working for.

'I want the bed at the end,' I said.

'You can't have it,' said Marise. 'You're in the middle and I'm the fire end and Poopy's the other end.'

I got thankfully into bed and lay watching

Poopy and Marise combing out their curls. Poopy had no difficulty. A few upward movements of the comb, two pats, and the operation was complete. Marise had more to do, for her hair when combed out sprang into what we called her Zulu mat. She had to take the hair strand by strand and give it a little twist to recurl it. She was finished at last and pattered across the room to put out the light.

Presently she spoke fretfully into the darkness. 'What's this mattress made of— straw?' she inquired.

'Mine smells musty,' I said. 'We ought to have aired them. Now we'll all get rheumatism.'

We listened to Kariman's grunts as she stretched herself on her mattress on the dressing-room floor.

'Do you suppose,' asked Poopy, 'that we'll get any servants?'

'Of course,' I said. 'I hope we'll get nice cheerful hill ones. In any case, Ali'll be here in a day or two. I would have asked for Yusuf, only I don't suppose my sisters would let him come.'

'If my father knew,' said Marise slowly, 'how I'm sleeping tonight, on a wet straw mattress in a room hanging in mid-air, he'd ...'

'You both owe me,' broke in Poopy, 'four rupees.'

'What on earth for?'

'Two thirds of a canary,' said Poopy.

I awoke to find sunshine flooding the balcony and sending bright shafts across the floor of the bedroom. I sat up in bed and remained for some moments transfixed at the sight of the snows, towering and majestic, the whole magnificent range visible. Poopy stirred and I jerked my chin towards the view.

'Look at that,' I said.

Poopy sat up and looked. 'We'll soon get used to it,' she said. 'Look at Marise. She sleeps with her head under the covers. I'd choke.'

The bulge that was Marise stirred; a hand appeared and pushed down the bedclothes, and a head appeared. Poopy and I looked at her and we both felt that this, too, was a lovely sight—Marise's skin, flushed to an unusual pinkness, her pale gold hair and vividly blue eyes, her soft little red mouth, even the frown she wore on waking.

'What's the time?' she asked.

'Look at the view,' I said.

Marise gave a great yawn, blinked, shook her head, and looked out. 'Brrr!' She gave a distasteful shiver. 'Snow on them. This room's like ice. Why can't that fat Kariman light a fire?'

Kariman, appearing indignantly, explained that lighting fires was no part of her work. She would wash our clothes, if there was any water and if someone would carry it upstairs. She would iron, if there was an iron and if there was a cook to heat it and a boy to bring it to her. She would dust those parts of the room that rested on solid foundations.

'Why don't you go back to Calcutta if you don't like it here?' I asked.

'Your mother,' said Kariman, 'she is dead. That way, I look after you. You think you big lady, but you only Miss-Sahib still.'

She went downstairs, presumably in search of food, and presently a sweeper, our own sweeper, brought hot water and poured it into the bathtubs. We got up, ready to face the day.

Cloma had promised to help us in our search for servants, but the morning brought aid from an unexpected source. Scarcely was breakfast over in the large room downstairs when Kariman came in and announced, a little doubtfully, that a gentleman had called to see us.

'See who?' asked Marise hopefully.

The gentleman had, it appeared, named me. I got up and walked into the little hall and stood looking in polite hesitation at the visitor. He waited patiently while I searched my mind for clues as to his identity. I was becoming more embarrassed as the moments went by, but the dark young man, leaning negligently against the front door, showed no signs of awkwardness.

'I'm awfully sorry,' I said. 'I don't ...'

'Oh my!' came a nasal, singsong drawl. 'Oh

132

my! You've forgotten me, but!'

My mouth opened, closed again, reopened. Of course! How could I have...

I gave a squeak and in an instant Poopy and Marise had joined me and were staring at the newcomer.

'Good heavens! Benny!' said Poopy.

'Benny! Mrs Knox, it's Benny. Benny de Souza,' I said, running back into the room. 'Do come. It's Benny. You remember?'

Mrs Knox came out and Miss Brooke followed.

We led Benny out of the dark hall, through the room, and into the glare of the veranda. We put him into a chair and sat round him, studying him as frankly as he studied us.

He was tall and thin and gangling. His eyes, once so full of earnestness, had now a lazy twinkle. It was not only the twinkle that was lazy, for Benny's whole attitude was one of carefree leisure. His clothes were terrible—a pair of shapeless grey flannel trousers, a khaki shirt, a tweed jacket lined with red material. His shoes were the old, familiar, dirty white tennis variety; his khaki topee looked as though an animal with very large teeth had worried it. Throughout the time he remained in Darjeeling, his outfit never varied.

His eyes roamed slowly over our circle. The human survey over, he began an architectural one. From his chair he could see the cracks, the frayed wicker furniture, the holes.

133

'You pay how much?' he inquired.

Mrs Knox told him, and Benny whistled slowly. 'That! Last year,' he said, 'the people only paid two hundred a month, and they got better stuff inside the house.' He shook his head regretfully. 'They always know,' he ended, 'what people they can do in the eye.'

Mrs Knox acknowledged the truth of this. 'We'll improve it by degrees,' she said. 'We'll buy a rug or two, and we'll hide those holes.'

'Benny,' I said suddenly, 'we've got no servants.'

Benny's eyes went to the figure of Kariman crossing the drawing room, and I told him that the others had gone.

'They cleared out?'

'Yes. We've got the sweeper who goes with the house, and we're getting Ali and we've got Kariman.'

'Kariman? What use,' asked Benny in astonishment, 'is that fat old ayah?'

'None,' I said. 'Can you do anything?'

Benny leaned back, tilting his chair dangerously. 'How many?' he asked.

'We want a cook,' said Mrs Knox. 'That's the most important. Then we need a bearer to work under Ali, a younger one to do odds and ends. That's three.'

'I'll send them,' promised Benny, 'this afternoon.'

He was as good as his word. At teatime Kariman, looking almost cheerful, announced that two men and a boy had arrived. Mrs Knox said that she would see them one at a time, beginning with the cook, and Kariman brought in a short, smiling Nepalese.

'Do you speak English?' asked Mrs Knox.

The man smiled—the wide, happy smile of the hillman. 'Berry good,' he said.

'Well, that's a relief,' said Mrs Knox. 'Have you brought your chits?'

The man burrowed inside his dilapidated jacket and produced a bundle of greasy papers. Mrs Knox took them gingerly and I came to the rescue.

'I'll read them for you,' I said.

I separated the dirty sheets and read one or two of the references.

'Why do you call him Susie?' asked Miss Brooke.

'That's what he's called here,' I said. 'S-u-s-i.'

'Oh. Well, Susi,' asked Mrs Knox, 'do you keep the cookhouse clean?'

Susi grinned rapturously. 'Berry good,' he said.

'I'll inspect it once a day,' said Mrs Knox. 'And I'll pay you thirty-five rupees a month.'

Susi bowed. 'Berry good,' he said.

He removed himself, and the man and the boy came in together. They were father and son, but the likeness between them was so striking and their sizes so exactly similar that they looked more like twins. The interview was

135

scarcely a success. They spoke no English and no Hindustani; we had no Bhutia or Nepalese. They produced a sheaf of recommendations so tattered as to be unreadable, and finally we were reduced to nodding our heads. We nodded at them to indicate that they would do, and they nodded back to indicate that we would do, too. Kariman ushered them towards the servants' quarters and sent Susi back to get orders for dinner.

'We'll have a simple dinner tonight,' said Mrs Knox. 'You can go to the bazaar tomorrow and get in a good stock of things.'

'Berry good,' said Susi.

'A little vegetable soup tonight,' went on Mrs Knox, 'cutlets with mashed potatoes, and a caramel custard. I hope you can make a good caramel custard?'

Susi's smile became wider. 'Berry good,' he said.

'Well, that's all,' said Mrs Knox. 'What time do you usually come back from the bazaar in the morning?'

'Berry good,' said Susi.

There was a pause. Mrs Knox spoke once more. 'Have you clean clothes?'

'Berry good,' said Susi.

'I don't believe,' said Mrs Knox, 'that you speak a single word of English.'

Susi's reply proved that he knew two.

'Well, go away,' said Mrs Knox. 'I only hope you can cook.'

Susi could cook very well. He sent in an excellent dinner—clear soup, Irish stew, and a very good prune mould.

CHAPTER THIRTEEN

A week after our arrival nobody would have recognized the inside of Landslide House. We had worked not only hard but systematically and had fallen more or less naturally into different spheres of industry. Miss Brooke had been revealed as the master mind; she knew exactly when to hide a hole with a picture and when to conceal it behind a graceful fern. She knew which chairs should be covered and which taken out on the balcony and painted. She marched down to the bazaar and came back followed by two and sometimes three coolies carrying her purchases. She demanded dirzees and Susi brought two. They sat cross-legged on the veranda and machined, and from cheap cotton materials there emerged dainty curtains, well-fitting covers, and five colored bedspreads, which brightened the bedrooms considerably.

Benny appeared daily. This, he told us, was the slack season in photography. When the visitors began to arrive, he would be busier. We hoped he would be busy in the meantime on our behalf, but he sat on a wicker chair on the veranda, his feet outstretched, his deplorable topee tilted over his eyes to keep out the glare, moving only when Ali carried out a tray of biscuits and lemonade.

With the house looking almost as charming as Cloma's, we began to feel at home. The evenings were very pleasant. Susi's cooking maintained its high standard, and after dinner we sat round on the newly covered chairs and read or talked. The only cloud on the horizon was the canary, Tom Cheep. He was well and cheerful, but not all Miss Brooke's efforts could coax out of him the songs he had sung so beautifully in Calcutta.

My father had arranged the hire of a piano for me and when it came things were even more pleasant. Marise was discovered to have a small but pretty soprano and sang unfamiliar French words to familiar English tunes. The only fault which might have been found during those evenings, a lack of masculine society, was soon to be remedied. Marise had a letter from Mr Creer saying that he would be up in Darjeeling before the end of the week and hoped to stay for a fortnight.

Benny urged us to visit the studio and have our photographs taken; less, we gathered, because he considered us good models than to give him something to do during his long, dull working days.

'There's nobody,' he complained. 'Since last month not a single one has come. I sit there and do what-all day after day, day after day. You girls come and I'll take your photos. You know where the studio is? Just beyond the bandstand on the Chowrusta you take that steep road for a little while and soon at a corner you come to the studio. You'll see the name.'

We saw it perfectly when we found our way there a day or two later. The name—*P. Rustomjee*—was painted on a board near the broken-down gate; it was written on another board nailed to a gatepost and scrawled in large white paint letters on three sides of the building; lest anybody should miss it, it was painted on the tin roof.

We walked along the stony drive to a wooden door. Marise knocked and then rattled the handle and, getting no reply, gave the wood a vigorous push. There was a splitting sound and the next moment the door swayed, came towards us, and fell flat on the ground, scattering us in panic to the grass banks at the side of the drive. We looked up to see Benny coming round the side of the building.

'Look at that,' he said in an exasperated tone. 'You've pulled the door out, you girls. Didn't you read the notice I put?'

He pointed and we saw behind us a cardboard notice propped up with two large stones. It read, *Other Way*.

'Well, which other way?' demanded Marise. 'That's the front door, isn't it?'

'It isn't working,' said Benny. 'That's why I put the notice. Purposely I put it, and then you come and pull out the door without noticing.'

'Well, are you going to leave it like that?' asked Poopy.

Benny stooped, picked up the door, and bore it back to its frame. After an anxious search he found the two nails which had been holding it up, and drove them in once more. He then conducted us through the side door into a tiny studio on whose walls hung samples of Mr Rustomjee's finest photographic studies.

'Who's first?' inquired Benny.

Marise was first, and as the preliminaries had taken longer than we anticipated, she was also the last. Benny disappeared behind the black cloth, came out again, whisked a cover off the lens, and put it back again. When he had repeated this performance four times, we had to hurry away.

The four photographs had a swift and direct influence upon Benny's future. He made several copies of the best photograph and took one to almost every little shop in the town and asked the owner to display it. Everybody was only too pleased to hang the lovely likeness with the name P. Rustomjee above it.

A fortnight passed, and Benny hurried up to Landslide House with great news.

'You know what's happened?' he asked. 'That photo I took of Marise—one chap from Calcutta saw it hanging in a shop and he came to the studio to see me. I didn't know who he was. How could I know, but? And what does he do? He knocks over the door like you girls. So I came out and I said to him, "Look, man, what do you use your eyes for? Can't you read that notice I put?" I was going on at him, and then I nailed the door up again and he helped me to do it, and then I said, "You want to be photoed?" and he said, "No, I'm from Lindrums." And I said, "You're standing here and saying nothing about where you come from, and you come from Lindrums!" And he said, "There's a photo in a shop up there—a girl's, and ..."'

'Oh Benny, he's going to give you a job!' I said.

'Wait on,' said Benny. 'I'm telling you. I told him I took the photo and he asked me lots of things—how old I am, how long I was in the studio and all that. And then he said they'd give me a job in ...'

'Oh, in Calcutta!' said Marise.

'No, not in Calcutta at first, because I have to learn more. I'm going to be in Allahabad first, where they have a branch, and then I can come and work in the Calcutta studio, that's what that chap said.'

We congratulated him heartily. He was to leave in a month, and his successor had already been appointed. He left us and hurried away to write the news to his family.

Poopy raised a question of more direct
141

interest to ourselves. 'What,' she asked, 'are we going to do about getting about?'

Transport was necessary. We were two miles away from the shops and nobody could expect us to walk two miles. Mrs Knox and Miss Brooke, both English-bred, might put on heavy boots and plod along the highways, but Poopy, Marise, and I thought walking dull.

'If you like,' said Poopy to Mrs Knox, 'we can arrange for you and Miss Brooke to have a rickshaw every day. If you make a contract with the men, it's cheaper than hiring one just when you want it.'

Miss Brooke shuddered. 'Not rickshaws, I think, thank you,' she said. 'I don't know whether it's my fault or the rickshaws', but I can't get comfortable in them. If I lean back, I feel as though I'm lying with my legs in the air; and if I lean forward, I feel certain I'm going to tumble out. And the poor men breathe so. Coming up the slope from the station they got wheezier and wheezier, and I was very much afraid they were going to have heart attacks. No, no rickshaws, thank you, unless this monsoon you talk about is so heavy that one can't get about.'

'No rickshaws,' said Poopy.

'If you don't walk,' asked Miss Brooke, 'how will you get about?'

'We're going to hire horses,' said Poopy. 'If you make a contract, it's cheaper than...'

'Horses? You don't mean,' said Miss

Brooke, 'those peculiar little ponies one sees, with little native boys and girls in charge of them?'

'Yes,' I said. 'They look a bit rickety, the ponies, but they're useful for getting about. We'll see about it tomorrow.'

We set out on the following day to strike a bargain, but we went by a circuitous route, for I was going to call on Miss Gumm on the way to fix the days for my lessons. We found the house easily. It was a large building called Marble Villa, divided exactly in two by its front door. The owner lived to the right of the door, Miss Gumm to the left.

Leaving Poopy and Marise to wait for me at the gate, I knocked on the common front door and a Nepalese servant led me along a narrow corridor and knocked at a door.

'In!' said the voice of Miss Gumm.

I was ushered inside and stopped on the threshold in astonishment. I had become used to Miss Gumm's collection of heads, but I had not expected her to bring them up to Darjeeling with her. The room was much smaller than her music room in Calcutta and though she had used every available inch of wall space, half the heads still remained unhung. They lay on chairs, on sofas, on the floor, on the piano; two barred my way into the room.

Stepping over them, Miss Gumm came towards me with outstretched hands. 'You haf

143

come to blay,' she told me.

I explained that I had merely come to settle the days for my lessons. Miss Gumm searched for her notebook, found it under a tiger skin, and decided that Mondays and Thursdays would suit her best.

I thanked her, clambered over the obstacles, and went out to join Poopy and Marise. We walked to the stables below the Mall and stood outside while the syces—diminutive girls, for the most part—led their mounts out for our inspection. It was too early in the season for visitors; the pick was ours. Poopy and Marise chose chestnuts and I picked out a cement-colored animal with dark spots.

'Not *that* one,' said Marise distastefully. 'He looks...'

'He looks quiet,' I said.

It was—and is—the one quality I desire in horse-flesh. Anybody can have the springy ones. I prefer the drooping, hopeless kind.

'What's its name?' I asked the little syce.

Its name was quite unpronounceable. We struck our bargain: so much a month and the horses to be brought to us every afternoon at two o'clock and collected at six, beginning tomorrow. We left the stable and walked slowly homeward, deciding as we went to name the horses after the neighboring territories—Nepal, Bhutan, and Sikkim. I was to have Sikkim.

On the following afternoon Nepal, Bhutan,

and Sikkim were brought round punctually at two. We all walked out to the side entrance and looked at them.

'They look all right,' said Poopy.

We looked all right ourselves. Poopy was the only one of us who had a riding kit and she had produced three pairs of jodhpurs—two good and one indifferent. We tossed for them and I got the indifferent pair, but with a fresh white blouse and a well-cut jacket, also borrowed from Poopy, I felt that I could figure in one of the more modest sports magazines. Miss Brooke gazed at the animals as though she was having some difficulty in placing the species.

'Horses,' I told her. 'Bhutan, Poopy's; Nepal, Marise's; Sikkim, mine.'

Sikkim gave me a friendly glance and I patted his nose.

'Can you all ride?' asked Miss Brooke.

'Poopy can,' I said. 'Marise says she can and I think I can. I can sit on any horse so long as it's standing.'

'But have you...'

'I stayed at a farm once,' I said. 'We'll be all right.'

We swung into our saddles with quite an air and as we did so, the three ponies, as if in response to a signal, walked to a grassy bank and began to tear off mouthfuls of grass.

'Hi, stop it!' said Marise. 'Come on—hup.'

Her pony ignored the appeal, and even Poopy's practised hands seemed unable to detach her mount from his juicy feed.

'This pony,' she said, 'hasn't any mouth at all. How about yours?'

'Well,' I said, 'I don't like to tug too hard. Come on! Gee up, Sikkim.'

He left the bank, swung round, peered for one awful moment over the edge of our precipice, and then bolted headlong through the gate. He elected to go uphill instead of down. I glanced at the ground, saw thankfully that it was not too far away, and gave my mind to the task of remaining in the saddle until Sikkim decided to stop.

It was an exhilarating ride and the first of many hair-raising expeditions. If there was an edge, Sikkim liked to walk along it. The sheerer, the nearer, seemed to be his motto. Like all hill ponies, he was sure-footed; like most, he ignored the rider and followed his own inclinations. If he wanted to go, he went; if he saw a nice bit of grass, he stopped to eat it. He chose precipitous paths up the face of a mountain and took them at a steady lope, flicking his tail contemptuously into the face of any passerby. Where he went, Bhutan and Nepal followed. Poopy averted her eyes from the more dreadful drops and Marise said prayers under her breath.

Mr Creer was almost due, and Marise raised the question of joining the club. The matter was put before Mrs Knox. She was in mourning and felt unable to help us, but Miss

146

Brooke said that though she was not prepared to make very much use of the club, she would join and propose us.

'I'm not keen,' said Poopy. 'What do we do there?'

'You can skate,' said Marise, 'and you can play tennis and you can dance. What more do you want?'

'Well, I'm not much good at tennis,' said Poopy, 'and I don't want to dance, because I don't know anybody to dance with, but I wouldn't mind skating.'

I wanted to play tennis. Marise wanted, chiefly, to have the right to enter the premises. If Mr Creer got out of her clutches and vanished into the club, she was not going to be debarred from going in and retrieving him. Miss Brooke therefore joined and soon afterwards Poopy, Marise, and I became temporary members and I found an amiable tennis marker willing to play with me.

Mr Creer arrived. Marise announced his arrival and asked Mrs Knox if he might come to dinner. He came and we were polite, but he was only to stay for a fortnight and we all had a feeling that he would be the first of many young men brought to the house by Marise. She had already tossed off the names of a half-dozen young men who were pressing her to dine and dance, to take tea at Vado's, or to go on one or more of the local excursions. When Mr Creer's vacation came to an end, the echoes of our farewell mingled with our greeting to another young man seeking refuge from Calcutta's heat and dust.

Benny left the day after Mr Creer, and we went down to the station to see him off. He stood by his luggage—a small tin trunk and a thin bedding roll—and we said good-by. Bidding farewell to Benny was never a sad performance; he regarded partings as natural and not to be grieved over. There was nothing to indicate that he would ever see us again and nothing in his bearing to show that the possibility distressed him. We laughed, he laughed, the coolies laughed. There were no awkward pauses and no tension. Before we had turned away for the last time, he was on his way to inspect the little engine and tell the driver how to run it.

'Can I wear one of your dresses?' Marise asked me when we were back at Landslide House. 'I'm going out with Mr Searle and he's seen all mine.'

'Which one?' I asked cautiously.

'The blue.'

'All right, but you'll have to send it to be cleaned tomorrow. You forgot last time.'

We helped her into it, pinned her shoulder straps, sent for a rickshaw, lent her Poopy's white evening bag, put her evening shoes into a shoe bag, powdered her back lightly, helped her into a little white evening coat borrowed from Miss Brooke, and saw her into a rickshaw. Poopy and I waved her off and stood for a little while in the darkness at the front gate.

'She looked nice, didn't she?' I said.

'She always does, specially when she's in our clothes. Hers are a bit fussy. Funny how she attracts all those men.'

'I don't think it's funny,' I said. 'I can't see how they can help it.'

'No. But looks are odd, in a way,' said Poopy thoughtfully. 'Look at your sisters. You wouldn't really call them outstanding, but look at the way your house was always cluttered up with all those men. And when Marise's men friends come here, you don't see them looking at you or me, do you?'

'Well, they wouldn't, would they, with Marise there,' I pointed out consolingly. 'But I think the funniest thing is that—really and honestly, Poopy—with all those men in Calcutta and all these of Marise's up here, I've never seen one I'd look at—even if he looked at me first, I mean.'

'Neither have I,' said Poopy. 'Most of them look rather alike to me. I can't say I've ever seen one I could be keen on.'

'Perhaps,' I said, 'if they showed they were awfully keen on us, we'd get keen on them.'

'No,' said Poopy, 'it isn't that. If they liked me, I'd like them even less. I suppose I'm the sort of girl that doesn't care much for men. Some are like that. I can't imagine myself ever

149

letting myself go over anybody like Marise does. I'd like to wait for years and then meet a sort of oldish man.'

We turned and walked slowly indoors and I thought over what Poopy had said and agreed with it all. She was not, I felt, the type of girl who would fall in love, at any rate until she was quite old.

And the following week she met William Lancaster and fell hopelessly, irretrievably, and irrevocably in love.

CHAPTER FOURTEEN

The appearance of William Lancaster among us was not quite unheralded. In one of Sir Guy's letters, written a few weeks earlier, he had mentioned one of his secretaries. He called him young Lancaster and told Poopy that he would be going up to Darjeeling on special duties in April and would be there for some months. He would, at Sir Guy's request, call on Poopy.

He called. It was about noon on a Sunday morning. Marise had been to Mass and Poopy and I had been to morning service. We were upstairs on our balcony sorting our laundry when Kariman came and told us that a gentleman was below waiting to see Poopy Miss-Sahib.

'Who is it, Poopy?' asked Marise.

'I don't know,' said Poopy. 'Come on. We'll all go.'

We all went, and when we entered the drawing room we saw a good-looking young man, sturdy rather than tall, with something about him that reminded me of a bull terrier, a firm and tenacious look. He was talking to Mrs Knox. He rose at our entrance and looked, a little hopefully, at Marise.

'This is Poopy,' said Mrs Knox.

Mr Lancaster's eyes went to her and he smiled. 'How d'you do?' he said. 'I promised your father I'd...'

'Yes,' said Poopy.

He was presented to Marise and to me, and with a slightly rueful smile he picked up two packages from the table and held them out to Poopy. 'I didn't exactly expect you to be in the nursery,' he said, 'but your father did rather give me the impression that you were—well...'

An engaging smile ended the speech and his glance indicated the presentation—a box of Turkish delight, a large tin of chocolates.

'That's all right for any age, isn't it?' asked Marise.

He laughed, and we were soon sitting on the veranda in the sunshine and Mrs Knox was apologizing because we had nothing in the way of what she termed a masculine drink to offer him. He told her that he had often wanted to find out what water tasted like, and a large jugful was brought out and we added our own flavorings and chattered. Poopy was silent, but as she was at no time a great talker, we scarcely noticed how little she contributed to the conversation.

Lunch time approached and Mrs Knox tendered an invitation to stay and have it with us.

Mr Lancaster, with a glance at his wrist watch, sprang to his feet in dismay. 'Great Scott!' he said. 'I've got to be at the club in ten minutes. I'd no idea how the time had gone!'

With the most charming regrets for being unable to stay he took his departure. Poopy, Marise, and I went to the gate with him and watched him go with long strides along the road.

'He's nice-looking, isn't he?' said Marise as we turned and went slowly indoors.

'I think he's taller than he looks,' I said. 'He's awfully broad and that makes him look sort of shorter. I like men with brown eyes and his are nice and twinkly, and I like his nose; it's nice and short and he's got a nice mouth.'

'Yes, his mouth was very nice,' said Miss Brooke at the end of this catalogue. 'He's a very pleasant young man altogether. You don't often get that combination of charm and reliability. I should say he'd been very well brought up.'

'His voice was nice, don't you think?' said Marise. 'He teases a bit. He says serious things

152

and then you see his eyes looking at you and laughing. I think he's nice. Do you like him, Poopy?'

There was no reply. Poopy was learning against one of the windows of the veranda, gazing out at the view.

'Poopy,' I said.

No reply. Poopy continued to gaze out of the window.

'Hey, Poopy!'

She turned and looked at me. 'Hm?' she asked.

'Don't dream, Poopy,' said Marise. 'We're talking about Mr Lancaster. We all like him, but after all he's your friend, so you ought to say what you thought of him.'

To our astonishment Poopy remained silent. Her eyes went from one to the other of us as we stood round and watched her, and we saw that there was a very strange expression in them.

After a moment Mrs Knox spoke a little uneasily. 'Well, Poopy?'

Poopy's voice came as flatly and as stolidly as ever. 'I think he's wonderful,' she said.

After our first surprise we laughed. 'Oh Poopy, my dear, not wonderful,' said Mrs Knox. 'Pleasant, charming...'

'I think he's wonderful,' said Poopy.

'Oh Poopy, don't be silly,' said Marise. 'I could show you dozens of men like that. If you'd go about with them more, you wouldn't think that the first man who comes to see you is

153

especially fascinating. Of course,' she admitted, 'I like Mr Lancaster.'

'I think he's wonderful,' droned Poopy.

We felt a little impatient. Fortunately, at this point Ali announced lunch and we walked inside and took our places round the table. By a kind of unspoken agreement, it was felt to be unwise to discuss Mr Lancaster any further, and Mrs Knox led the talk into safer channels. Poopy, however, had nothing to say. She ate as heartily as usual, but she appeared to be dreaming.

Soon Marise's irritation got the better of her. 'Poopy,' she said, 'why're you mooning?'

She had to repeat it twice, and then Poopy answered simply. 'I was thinking of Mr Lancaster,' she said.

'Well, don't keep on thinking of him,' said Marise. 'It's silly. You can think of him later, if you think he's so beautiful.'

'I think he's...'

'Wonderful,' finished Marise. 'If you say it again, we'll all scream out loud. Won't we, Mrs Knox? And it isn't the thing,' she went on irritably. 'It isn't the thing at all. You should keep your feelings to yourself.'

'Why?' asked Poopy. 'Just because I think he's...'

'No!' shouted Marise, to the astonishment of the bearer who was handing her the peas. He removed the dish hastily and Marise was obliged to call him back.

'I don't see,' said Poopy, 'why you're cross.'

'You've often told her,' I put in, 'that she ought to notice men more. Now just because she's noticing one, you're angry with her.'

'I am not angry with her,' said Marise. 'I am pleased, very pleased. This is the first time she has seen a man she likes. So far, that's good. But if she behaves stupidly with us, if she shows us so openly that she's—that she's...'

'Bowled over.'

Marise thanked me with a look. 'Bowled over. If she shows us, then she'll show him and that will be wrong. Ask Mrs Knox. Won't it be wrong, Mrs Knox?'

'Perhaps it would be wrong for Poopy to tell him she thinks he's...'

'Yes, yes, don't start her off again,' begged Marise. 'All I ask is for Poopy to like him just as much but not to show it, because if she does...'

She paused, her shoulders up, her hands outspread. I saw amusement in the eyes of Mrs Knox and Miss Brooke, but they said nothing. Marise was acknowledged to be mistress of the subject.

She said no more until the three of us were curled up on chairs on our balcony after lunch. We did not ride on Sundays. Poopy seemed lost in dreams, and after a while Marise addressed her. 'Do you really like him, Poopy?' she asked.

'Yes,' said Poopy. 'I think he's...'

155

'All right,' said Marise. 'Then you must listen to me. Next time he comes you must talk. You mustn't just sit as you did this morning, looking partly lunatic. Just be like you always are. And when he comes next time...'

The lesson went on, but there was, alas, no next time. The week went by, another week came and went, and we saw nothing of Mr Lancaster. An uneasy conviction crept into our minds. Mr Lancaster had done his duty, visited his chief's daughter, made his bow, left his compliments and Turkish delight—and gone. Only Marise remained hopeful. She pointed out that he was a sensible man, and a sensible man would call more than once upon the daughter of somebody upon whom his future promotion depended. If he didn't come for Poopy's sake, she argued, he would come for his own.

He didn't, however, come at all. Nothing was heard of him until Marise came home one evening and reported that she had seen him dancing at the club. Worse, he had been dancing with the Misses Greenstone. Marise, unable to bear the sight, had neglected her own party and by a clever coup had made him dance the last three dances with her. Her friends had not liked it; the Greenstones had liked it even less, but she had done it for Poopy.

Poopy was grateful but hopeless. 'Then he won't come any more,' she said.

'Left to himself, perhaps not,' admitted

156

Marise. 'But if he's asked, then he'll have to come. We must get Mrs Knox to ask him.'

Mrs Knox wrote a note—would Mr Lancaster dine on Friday evening? Mr Lancaster replied that he would, and we prepared for the great day. Miss Brooke, after consultation with us, drew up a suitable menu and, determined that this time Susi should follow our instructions, sketched on a large sheet of paper the ingredients necessary for each dish. She drew and colored a steaming tureen of soup with tomatoes beside it; below it were little individual dishes surrounded by fish and a carton of cream. Next came a charming sketch of a duck and some pea pods and last, a soufflé dish and a large cheese. We called Susi in and it was obvious from his delight and his intelligent exclamations that he could follow the pictures perfectly.

We discussed the question of asking another man or two. Mrs Knox felt that it would balance the party, but Marise was against it. She could, she said, bring several men. There was this one in the Police, that one in the Hongkong and Shanghai Bank, two more in the Indian Civil Service. They waited only for an invitation from her, but with Mr Lancaster alone it would seem more like an intimate family party.

We dressed with care. Marise and I made our own toilettes before allowing Poopy to dress. We knew by experience that even ten

157

minutes was enough for her clothes to get into disorder. I wore a long white dress with a blue sash and felt rather schoolgirlish, but my blue was at the cleaner's and Marise was wearing my green. She borrowed it with a resigned air. It was clear that she was wearing it because it was the plainest dress we had and in it she would not put Poopy in the shade.

Poopy looked beautiful when we had done with her. When we went downstairs, her appearance drew unwonted compliments from both Mrs Knox and her sister. We knew that Poopy was nervous, but from her calm expression—or lack of it—nobody would have imagined that she was feeling the pangs of first love.

The evening was not a success. The dinner was very good—Susi's best Julienne soup, something very tasty in aspic jelly, roast chicken, and a cream tower, another Susi specialty. There was asparagus with a delicate sauce. There were even masculine drinks for the guest, but as he drank them we felt that there were too many women in the party. Mr Lancaster was charming. Miss Brooke was amusing and no table at which Mrs Knox sat could lack good conversation. Outwardly all was smooth, but I was not happy and I knew from an occasional crease in Marise's smooth brow that something was missing.

Some time after dinner Mrs Knox asked me to play. I chose my shortest, my lightest piece and tripped through it, but in the piano's glossy surface I saw the guest steal a look at his watch.

When I had finished, Mrs Knox looked at Marise. 'Marise, my dear,' she said, 'won't you sing that...'

Before the sentence could be completed, Mr Lancaster was on his feet. 'By Jove!' he exclaimed. 'I'd no idea the time had gone so quickly. I really must be off!'

He was off, and the speed of his departure made me wonder whether he was anxious to avoid being drawn into another engagement. Poopy expressed no opinion as to the success of the evening. Mrs Knox and her sister thought everything had gone very well, and Marise agreed with them.

Up in our own room, however, she abandoned pretense. 'We mustn't ask him again,' she said. 'It wasn't... he didn't enjoy it.'

'I know,' said Poopy.

'Well, don't look like that,' said Marise, though a stranger would have thought that Poopy was looking just as usual. 'It isn't the end, you know. You've just got to think of something he'll like to do. He doesn't like being indoors, I suppose.'

She stopped talking and appeared to ponder. Poopy undressed slowly and silently. Kariman shuffled in from the dressing room and asked if we wanted anything.

'No, go to sleep,' I said.

She retired thankfully and Marise, peeling off my dress and leaving it on the floor, addressed Poopy urgently. 'I think I know what to do,' she said. 'We oughtn't to have asked him here. What is there, after all? Two old women, even though they're nice, and just her and you and me. Even if he wanted to see you, he would have to see the other four as well, and he finds that dull. Just to sit and talk isn't very exciting. He wants to be active. He's young; he wants to dance.'

'I'm no good at dancing,' said Poopy. 'I never know what they're trying to do.'

'It's easy if you'll only try,' said Marise. 'A girl doesn't have anything to do. The man does everything. His legs move, your legs move. He goes, you go. He turns, you turn. If you come to dances, you can ...'

'No,' said Poopy. 'My legs don't go. I've tried.'

'Well then,' said Marise without hesitation, 'you'll have to ride with him. That's what you do best, after all. We'll ask him to ride with us. He'll enjoy it and ...'

'Supposing he doesn't come,' said Poopy.

Marise made a sound of exasperation. 'See here, Poopy,' she said. 'In a thing like this you don't say, suppose this and suppose that. You like this man, don't you?'

'I think he's ...'

'Yes, all right,' said Marise. 'You like him. He's handsome and strong, and so other girls will like him too. If you had seen that fatter Greenstone making cow's eyes at him, you'd know that if you want him to like you, you can't just sit on a bed like you're doing now, looking as if your mother had died. You...'

'Well, she...'

'Yes, I know. She did die. But are you just going to sit or will you do what I tell you to do?'

'Go on,' said Poopy.

'Well, we'll see if we can get him out riding,' said Marise.

In a little over a week Poopy wrote, at Marise's dictation, a short note to Mr Lancaster. We three were taking lunch and riding up to Ghoom. Would he care to come? We chose a Saturday when he might be free, and we chose Ghoom because three of Marise's dancing partners were going down that day in the Toy Train, and at Ghoom we could watch the train go round the horseshoe loop and wave to the departing swains.

Mr Lancaster wrote a noncommittal reply. He would very much like to come, but had not yet trusted himself to one of the hill ponies. It would perhaps be better if a little later...

At this, we rode to the stables and spoke seriously to our three syces. A gentleman, we said, was coming out with us, a fairly large gentleman. We required a good pony, a large pony, so that the gentleman's legs would not dangle. We looked at every pony in the stable and chose a bony animal somewhat taller than

161

our own.

'What's his name?' asked Poopy.

The syce seemed uncertain, so we christened him Obadiah and sent him to Mr Lancaster's office with a simple note. 'This is Obadiah. Please try him.'

We met on the Mall on Saturday morning, a morning full of sunshine and exhilaration. There was no doubt that we were a well-turned-out trio, and Mr Lancaster looked at us with the first sign of appreciation he had as yet shown. We started out four abreast. As the road narrowed, Marise sent me ahead with Mr Lancaster and followed with Poopy. In this formation we climbed slowly up the road to Ghoom, and our spirits rose as we went. At the second mile we were humming; at the third we had broken into song.

We reached what we considered the perfect spot for lunch and Mr Lancaster called a halt. 'This looks like it,' he said. 'The world at our feet—look at it. Will one of you get me off this horse? My legs feel wooden.'

We dismounted and led the ponies into a dip from which they could not wander. We untied the packages of lunch and settled down hungrily to sandwiches, hard-boiled eggs, and some of Susi's light pastry. We become more and more companionable, and by the time we were at the horseshoe bend and saw the train puffing into sight, we were able to give the waving and shouting gentlemen a very good send-off.

We turned homeward, and in the most natural way possible Marise and I took the lead. We went back as far as the stable and left Mr Lancaster there to pay for Obadiah. 'That was wonderful,' he said. 'We must do it again.'

We did it many times more. Mr Lancaster, finding himself at leisure, would send a grinning peon round with a note addressed to 'Those Young Ladies,' suggesting a ride. Sometimes he brought the meals, sometimes we did. Sometimes on the longer expeditions Mrs Knox and Miss Brooke accompanied us on foot or in rickshaws. We went up the mountains and down in the valleys. The days were bright and warm, the views perfect. The only expedition we fought shy of was the one made daily by tourists at this time of the year— the journey to Tiger Hill to watch the sun rise over Mount Everest. This meant rising at three o'clock in the morning and riding through the chill darkness. We often made up our minds to go, but the order to call us at three never seemed to be actually given.

One night I was awakened by Kariman shaking me urgently. I sat up and shook the sleep out of my eyes and stared at her with rising fear. There must be very bad news to necessitate her calling me in the dead of night.

'What's happened?' I said. 'Bad news?'

Kariman shook her head and put up a hand to indicate the need for quiet. 'No bad news,' she whispered. 'You get up.'

'Get up?' I stared at her uncomprehendingly. 'Get up?' There must, I thought, be an earthquake. My eyes went to the light to see if it was swinging, but I saw that it hung motionless.

'What's the matter with you?' I asked in an irritable undertone. 'There's no earthquake and there's no bad news. Are you ill?'

'Not ill. You get up,' urged Kariman. 'The Sahib downstairs, outside.'

'Sahib? What Sahib?'

'Lancaster Sahib. He say you all go Tiger Hill. He wait for you. You get up and I wake the other Miss-Sahibs.'

'You'll do nothing of the sort,' I said furiously. 'What sort of joke is this? What's the time?'

'There's no joke. Three o'clock,' said Kariman. 'Lancaster Sahib tell Knox Mem-Sahib that the Miss-Sahibs never go Tiger Hill, and he say one night he will come and bring ponies to take you.'

I leaned over and prodded Poopy and she stirred uneasily. 'Get up, Poopy,' I said softly. 'Mr Lancaster's downstairs—outside, I mean.'

Poopy sat up and stared. 'Something's happened,' she said.

'No, nothing. But he must have given Kariman a few hundred rupees to get her up at this...'

'No hundred rupees,' put in Kariman in an

164

indignant undertone. 'Only few rupees and . . .'

'Well, this is his way of making us go to Tiger Hill,' I said. 'Do you want to go? I don't. I bet Marise doesn't want to either. Shall I wake her?'

'You'd better,' said Poopy.

We woke Marise with a great deal of difficulty. When we had succeeded in making her understand that it was three o'clock and that she was expected to get up and dress and make a journey into the dawn, she slipped indignantly down into her bed, leaving an angry face glaring over the bedclothes.

'Go away,' she ordered Kariman. 'I won't go anywhere. Tell the Sahib to go away at once.'

She turned a shoulder to us, wriggled herself into a comfortable position, and took no further interest in the affair.

'I don't want to go, Poopy,' I said. 'Would it be all right if you went alone?'

'I think somebody ought to go,' said Poopy. 'I wish he'd asked me beforehand.'

I said nothing, remembering that he had asked us several times. Poopy got slowly out of bed. 'Go and tell the Sahib,' she said, 'that I'll come.'

'No other Miss-Sahibs?' inquired Kariman. 'The Sahib bring ponies.'

'Well, tell him to send them away,' I said, settling myself more comfortably between the sheets.

'It'll be a wonderful view,' said Poopy. 'Why

don't you come?'

'Don't want to,' I said. 'I can see wonderful views without losing any sleep.'

'But you can't see Mount Everest, only Kinchinjunga and the others.'

'They'll do. Hurry, Poopy, or he'll start throwing stones up or something.'

Poopy dressed hurriedly. Kariman, with a grunt, watched her go softly downstairs and then returned to her dressing room. I heard the sound of horses' hoofs, and before they died away I was asleep.

Mr Lancaster brought Poopy back to a late breakfast and ate it with her.

He looked with contempt at Marise and me. 'You'll never get another chance like that,' he said. 'No mist, nothing to hide the incomparable sight. We were ... well, spellbound is the word.' Mr Lancaster leaned over for the sugar basin and poured a liberal supply on his porridge. 'The colors!' he went on. 'I can't describe them, can you, Poopy? First the darkness and then the gradual lightening, then the first of the delicate colors and then the outline of the highest mountain in the world. Pass the milk, would you? Thanks. It was awe-inspiring. I've seen sights, but if I live to be one hundred I won't see another like that. The peaks came into sight...'

'Thank you,' said Marise. 'We've read about it.'

Mr Lancaster finished his eggs and bacon

and helped himself to the tinned sausages thoughtfully added to the meal by Susi. Having scraped the last of the mashed potatoes from the dish and squeezed the last drops of coffee from the pot, he wiped his mouth, sighed with content, and rose to go.

'I'm sorry to rush off straight from the table,' he said, 'but my minions await me.' He waved a general farewell and addressed Poopy. 'Thursday about three,' he said. 'Don't be late.'

He had gone. Marise and I followed Poopy upstairs and sat on our beds watching her take off her riding clothes.

'What did he mean about Thursday?' said Marise.

'He wants to take me to Lebong to see some people he knows there,' said Poopy.

'Didn't he ask us?'

'I don't think so, but if you want to come I don't see why you shouldn't. We've always gone in a bunch before,' said Poopy.

'Well, we won't go in a bunch again,' said Marise.

Poopy sank upon her bed and yawned.

'Was it worth getting up for, Poopy?' I asked. 'I mean, is the view as wonderful as they say?'

Poopy rubbed her nose. 'I don't know,' she said. 'We sat there and sat there, and when it was dawn a mist came up and you couldn't see anything at all. Just mist. No colors, no anything—just mist.'

We stared at her.

'B-but Mr Lancaster,' began Marise, 'said ... he said ...'

'Well, yes. He put it awfully well, didn't he?' said Poopy.

'I think he's a liar,' said Marise indignantly.

'I think he's wonderful,' said Poopy, before anybody could stop her.

CHAPTER FIFTEEN

The sight of Poopy and Mr Lancaster walking, riding, and even dancing together gave us all a great deal of satisfaction. To Marise especially it was a matter for self-congratulation. Left to himself, Mr Lancaster would have drifted out of our reach. She had used a little womanly wit and here he was on easy, brotherly terms with us all—at ease, dropping in and out when he chose and treating Poopy with the same teasing familiarity as he did the rest of us. We called him, at his earnest request, Bill. Mrs Knox and Miss Brooke approved of him thoroughly, and Mrs Knox felt no uneasiness over his friendship with Poopy. Had not Sir Guy himself sent Bill?

Poopy's happy state had, after a time, the effect of making Marise restless. Bill's companionship had one advantage denied to her: it was continuous, spreading over the fine months and going on into the monsoon and even longer. Bill would not, like her own young men, be able to devote but a brief fortnight to the ripening of the acquaintance. He was permanent, while her own dancing partners vanished after a week or two of vacation. Her successes were easy but they lacked continuity. Where, she asked us, could she find somebody like Bill, someone who was working in Darjeeling, someone who was not a mere bird of passage, someone who would not be torn away, leaving her to go through the same routine again and again? Where?

Poopy and I did our best, but we could think of no permanent young men who were free to attach themselves to Marise. Bill's colleagues were older than he, and married. All the bankers we knew were family men. Poopy thought that the only thing left was tea. We were surrounded by vast tea estates. On one of them there would surely be a Bill.

'Can't you walk past the Planters' Club and sort of glance at them?' suggested Poopy. 'You can see the veranda from the road.'

Marise walked and glanced and reported dejectedly that nothing on the veranda was a day under forty.

'That's no use,' said Poopy. 'There's the Military.'

'Half of them miles away at Lebong,' said Marise, 'and the other half stuck up miles away at Jalapahar. No.'

'Well, we'll all look around,' promised Poopy.

While we were looking round, Maurice Leete came into our lives. He came with the monsoon.

The rains had come early, and Bill, bringing Poopy back from a ride wet to the skin, besought her to get herself a mackintosh. Poopy went out when the downpour ceased and came back with a waterproof which caused Marise to give a cry of despair.

'Where, where, *where* did you get that thing?' she demanded. 'Oh Poopy, it's terrible! You should have waited for me to come home and I would have gone with you. No! You shan't keep it. Come with me and we'll take it back this minute and get you something you can look nice in.'

I went with them. None of us owned a mackintosh and the first rain had reminded us of what monsoon conditions could be. Marise chose a plain riding mackintosh for Poopy and after some search got a becoming little sou'wester to match. She put them on Poopy and looked at her with satisfaction.

'Now you look nice,' she said. 'Sensible and nice. You can be rained on a lot and still look dry and nice.'

She chose one for herself and looked critically at the one I had bought. 'You really like that?' she asked.

'What's the matter with it?'

'Well ... perhaps it'll do. Some people look better in mackintoshes than others. Try on that other one there and...'

'No. I've bought this and I think it looks nice. Well, fairly nice.'

Marise shrugged and forgot the matter. We left her in the shop. Poopy was going to walk home past Bill's office, dropping in to ask his approval of the mackintosh. I was going to Miss Gumm's. When I got home an hour later, Marise was sitting downstairs with Mrs Knox and Miss Brooke. On the chair which we now called Bill's sat a young man. He got up at my entrance and Marise introduced him as Mr Leete. Though I knew nothing else about him, a slight purr in her voice told me one thing—he was no bird of passage. He was permament.

He was, in fact, on the Leboongi Tea Estate. He was twenty-three, tall, rather thin, with a gentle voice and manner. He had met Marise at a dance a few nights earlier. Poopy and I, after studying him for some time, agreed that if there had been a sequel written to *Little Lord Fauntleroy*, Mr Leete could have posed as its hero.

'I don't mean,' Poopy added hastily, 'anything unkind.'

'Nor do I,' I said. 'I like him. But he *is* rather too gentle for a man. He...'

'It isn't him so much,' said Poopy reflectively. 'You feel when you look at him

171

that when he was young his mother dressed him in curls and velvet collars. He isn't exactly girlish. In fact, he isn't girlish at all, but he's ... well, he's the exact opposite to Bill.'

Perhaps this was why the two men got on well together. Bill was able to visit us more often than Maurice, but when the latter came up from the tea garden, the drawing room of Landslide House was filled by a happy group— Mrs Knox and her sister in deep chairs, Poopy, Marise, and I curled up anywhere, and the two men comfortable on the only two chairs with leg rests.

When they were not with us, our time was fully taken up with other important matters. This was the rainy season and we were indoors a great deal, but we had plenty to do. We had found a first-class dirzee and every chair in our bedroom held bundles of dress material. Sample snippets sent up from Calcutta by my sisters littered the table.

We looked through every fashion magazine we could buy or beg from Cloma. Tiring of magazines, I sketched some of my own ideas and got the dirzee to make them up for me. The dresses were a great success and the fact that they looked better on Marise and Poopy in no way detracted from my triumph. Especially admired was the pale blue day dress trimmed with white braid. It had a simple effectiveness that surprised us all.

Darjeeling was resting on white clouds. We

could see them below us and watched them rising, screening each peak and promontory as they rose. Presently they crept softly up our side road. The gate vanished; a wreath of mist came in at our ever-open window and played round Poopy's head. The balcony and the bedroom were filled with curling little wreaths; we saw one another like wraiths moving eerily through a fog.

It was too much for Kariman's spirits; a gloom descended upon her and she spent a good deal of time groaning. How, she asked, could anybody live in this vapor bath? For the fortieth time I offered her the fare to Calcutta; for the fortieth time she refused.

Everybody but Kariman was happy. Between Poopy and Bill there was a quiet, easy companionship. Maurice was deeply, openly in love and Marise treated him with firm kindness. Mrs Knox and Miss Brooke felt none of the depression which the perpetual mists aroused in lesser spirits. I only wanted one thing to make me really contented and I got it—a letter from my father saying that he was coming up on a visit.

With this letter came one from the elder of my sisters. I opened it on the veranda. It had not been a large mail and I was the last to finish, so that my startled exclamation found everyone at leisure to inquire into its reason.

'It's my big sister,' I explained. 'She says she's engaged!'

There was a general outcry of surprise, joy, and congratulation.

'Who is it?' asked Mrs Knox.

I studied the letter, which was from the more illiterate of my sisters. 'I think,' I said at last, 'his name's Olaf.'

'Olaf? Olaf? I never heard you mention any Olaf,' said Marise.

'Well, I didn't know any,' I said. 'My sisters knew a lot of men, but I didn't always get hold of their names, and I certainly never heard of an Olaf among them.'

'May I see?' asked Mrs Knox.

I gave her the letter and she handed it round. Everybody examined the bold circle, the unmistakable *l* following it, the hieroglyphic at the end. Bill thought that if it looked like anything it looked like Olaf.

'She's coming up with my father,' I said, 'and he—Olaf, I mean—is coming too. Next week. They're all going to the Mount Everest Hotel.'

'I must write and congratulate her,' said Mrs Knox.

We all wrote and expressed our pleasure at the prospect of meeting Olaf the following week.

My sister's reply to me bordered on the abusive. If I couldn't read, she said, I ought to learn. If my sight was defective, there were oculists. If I was trying to be rude about her writing, I ought to take a look at my own before spreading silly stories among my friends. She had, she informed me, never heard of an Olaf anywhere or at any time. Her fiancé was named C-l-i-v-e and, in case that didn't convey it clearly, it was CLIVE. His surname, she said was Nash. N for noble, A for Apollo, S for swoon, and H for heartbeat—NASH. To rhyme with *dash*.

I communicated this briefly to the others and we waited eagerly for the day which would bring my father, my sister, and the man we still spoke of as Olaf. They arrived in a break in the rains. Poopy and Marise went with me to the station to meet the little train, and they got a first glimpse of Olaf as I rushed at my father to greet him.

We sent the luggage to the hotel and walked slowly to Landslide House, taking surreptitious looks at the tall, fair man walking beside my sister. He seemed pleasant but, like Maurice Leete, he seemed a little too gentle.

Poopy and Marise left us near the club. I took the others on and soon we were at the house and Mrs Knox and her sister were welcoming the travelers. I left my father to talk to them and led my sister and her fiancé upstairs to show them our balcony. The snows were not visible, but we could see a good way ahead.

'Do you all sleep in that bedroom?' asked my sister, nodding towards it.

'Yes.'

'Don't you ever get tired of always being with the other two?'

'Poopy and Marise? No, of course not. I like it.'

'Who,' asked my sister, 'is the man Poopy's got hold of? The other one I'm not surprised about—Marise, I mean. She always had men trailing about after her, but I can't imagine anybody...'

'Poopy,' I broke in, 'is jolly attractive.'

'Attractive? Did you,' asked my sister, turning to her fiancé, 'did you think her attractive?'

'Which one?' asked Clive.

'There!' I said. 'If he doesn't know which one, then that means yes, because even you have to admit that Marise is...'

'Oh, Marise,' conceded my sister, 'is attractive. We all know that. And I suppose Poopy's got the usual eyes and nose and...'

'She's jolly nice,' I said hotly. 'You've never said so, not all her life, but she is. She...'

'She hasn't,' said my sister, 'one spark of expression in the whole of her face.'

'She has!'

'She hasn't!'

'She has!'

'Her face,' said my sister, 'always looks as though it got frozen like that and she could never move it again. It looks...' She paused, waiting for the right word. If she had waited twenty years America would have sent it to her—dead-pan.

'Just because she doesn't giggle all the time like you,' I said furiously, 'you think she can't laugh. Just because she...'

'This view,' said Clive, 'is really awfully...'

'Because she doesn't talk, talk, talk all the time,' I swept on, 'you think she's dull. Just...'

'She *is* dull,' said my sister. 'You might feel...'

'I don't feel anything,' I said. 'I only know that you've always run her down and...'

'I say,' put in Clive, 'this balcony doesn't...'

'And you've never admitted that she's...'

'You can't,' said my sister, 'admit what isn't there.'

'It *is* there!'

'It isn't!'

'This balcony,' said Clive, 'seems very unsteady.'

'Unsteady?' My sister gave a tentative stamp or two.

'Oh goodness!' I said. 'Don't do that!'

'Why not?'

'There's nothing underneath,' I said. 'If you go and look over, you'll see what I mean. We're sort of sticking out into the air and...'

I stopped. My sister had looked over and when she drew her head inside once more, the look on her face and its pallor caused Clive to move towards her with an evident intention of supporting her in his arms. I left them and went downstairs hurriedly.

Their visit passed more pleasantly than it had begun. Everybody liked my father, nobody found anything to say against Clive, and Bill and Maurice even liked my sister.

Before my father went back to Calcutta he made polite inquiries about Poopy and Marise. 'Your friends,' he said, 'appear to be equipped with cavaliers.'

'Yes, they're both nice, aren't they?' I said.

'They appear so,' said my father. 'Would it be discreet to ask how far the affairs have progressed?'

I considered. 'Well, I don't know,' I said at last. 'I hadn't thought much about that. I suppose Maurice has proposed to Marise—they always do. She doesn't say much, but sometimes he looks sad, as though she'd just said no.'

'I see,' said my father. 'And Poopy?' This was more difficult.

'I don't know,' I said slowly. 'Somehow Poopy isn't like Marise. I think that if Bill said anything she'd tell me. I used to think that he was only friendly, just as he was with Marise and me, but lately I don't think so. You know why?'

My father didn't.

'Well,' I said, 'a funny thing happened just before you came up. Bill was just going out with Poopy and we were downstairs and Marise was going upstairs, and as she passed Poopy she stopped and frowned a bit and settled her dress—Poopy's dress. You know how Poopy's things always seem to be falling off?'

'Yes, I know.'

'And how Marise and I and even Mrs Knox sometimes settle her pleats or her shoulder straps or her belt? I mean, we don't even think about it—it's just automatic. We've always done it and Poopy never even notices. She didn't notice this time either. Marise just said, "Oh, *Poopy!*" as we always do, and tweaked her dress into position and then went on upstairs. I thought nothing about it and then suddenly I saw Bill's face.'

'Well?'

'He was standing with an awful frown on his face, staring at the staircase where Marise had just gone up. He looked ... somehow he looked as though he'd have liked to sort of ... sort of kick her. Then he looked at Poopy for a minute or two and walked slowly towards her and put out his hand and put her dress back exactly as it had been before. Poopy looked a bit puzzled and said, "What did you do that for?" and Bill said, "Because *I*," and he sort of underlined the I, "because *I* like you just as you are." Does that,' I asked, 'mean anything special, do you think?'

'If we wait,' said my father, 'we shall see.' He gave a sigh, and pulled my hair absently. 'Young men all over the place,' he said. 'Your other sister looks like going off soon and then,

I suppose, it'll be your turn.'

I wondered. Perhaps, I reflected a little uneasily, I should have to devote myself to music after all.

CHAPTER SIXTEEN

A few days after the visitors went back to Calcutta, Bill came for dinner and passed Marise as she went out to meet Maurice and dine with him.

Bill bowed her out and, sitting on a long chair in the veranda, accepted a drink at Ali's hands. Mrs Knox and Miss Brooke were not yet dressed, and Poopy and I sipped our orange juice and waited for them.

'What did Marise think of the news?' Bill asked.

We stared at him. 'What news?'

It was Bill's turn to look surprised. 'Didn't Maurice,' he asked, 'come round this afternoon?'

'Yes,' I said. 'Ali said he came, but we were all out. Why did he come? He'd told Marise he couldn't see her until dinner.'

Bill put his drink down and looked at us. 'He came,' he said, 'to tell her the news.'

'What news?' demanded Poopy. 'You always take such a long time telling anything. What news?'

'About his mother,' said Bill. 'She's coming out.'

There was silence. They were three simple words, but they could mean anything. Maurice's mother was coming out. Darjeeling was a place that drew tourists from farther away than Maurice's home in Sussex. It was unusual for sightseers to choose the monsoon, but this visitor had more than the snows to draw her. Her only son was here.

Her only son—and she was coming out. An uneasiness, faint as yet, crept into my mind.

'What,' I heard Poopy say, 'is she coming out for?'

Bill lit a cigarette, leaned back, and inhaled. 'You know,' he said, 'as well as I do. She's been getting letters grinding away on one subject, and the maternal nose is twitching. The maternal nose wants to smell out this situation.'

'Maurice is twenty-four,' said Poopy. 'How can a mother run after a man of twenty-four like that? He's his own master, isn't he?'

'I wouldn't say so,' said Bill.

'You mean,' I asked, 'that he's a sort of a—a mother's boy?'

'Not quite,' said Bill.

'You mean,' said Poopy, 'that she's coming to poke her nose into our affairs.'

Bill looked at her. '"Our affairs,"' he repeated. 'I see. This isn't going to be a private fight?'

'If you'd talk sensibly,' said Poopy with a touch of irritation, 'we'd be able to find out whether it's going to be a fight at all.'

'This Mrs Leete,' I said, 'ought to be jolly glad her son's got hold of somebody as lovely as Marise.'

'She isn't "this Mrs Leete,"' said Bill. 'She's Lady Edwina Leete.'

'Lady? But she can't be,' said Poopy. 'I've heard people ask Maurice about his father and they call him Mister.'

'His father's Mr Leete,' said Bill, 'but he married an earl's daughter. Maurice would be an earl some day, if nine or ten—I'm not sure which—with a prior claim to the title got polished off first. Has this Marise of yours any idea what she's up against?'

'What,' asked Poopy, 'is she up against?'

'Quite a lot,' said Bill. 'She's taken a bite out of a rather rich cake. Did you two ever play tiddlywinks? Well, then, you know that whoever can get the most counters into the little pot gets the prize. Lady Edwina pops in an earl, a family tree with golden branches, a country seat, and ancestors who fought with or without William the Conqueror. We up here don't give much thought to the kind of background Lady Edwina's coming out full of. The moment she arrives, she'll be popping those things into the pot. Now you two tell me what you're going to pop in as a countermeasure.'

We were saved the necessity of attempting to tell him, for just then Mrs Knox and Miss Brooke joined us on the veranda. We went in to dinner, and throughout the meal Poopy and I were rather silent and absorbed, for we were busy playing tiddlywinks with Lady Edwina.

After dinner Bill addressed a casual remark to Mrs Knox. 'Before you came in this evening,' he said, 'I was telling the girls that Maurice's mother is on her way out.'

Mrs Knox raised her eyebrows. 'Out to India? Do you mean she's coming to visit Maurice?'

'Yes. He got the news this afternoon.'

'When he got the letter,' put in Poopy suddenly, 'what did he say? Was he ... well, how did he behave?'

Bill eyed her. 'Behave? Oh, he seemed quite touched,' he said. 'Jumped out of his chair and waved the letter over his head and said, "What fun, what fun! My mummy's coming to..."'

'Oh!' Poopy made a sound of disgust and we laughed.

'Joking aside,' said Mrs Knox, 'he must be very happy. I imagine he must be a rather charming son, and I feel she must be a nice woman to have a son like him.'

'These two,' said Bill, pointing with his pipe, 'think she's on her way out to separate the couple they've taken such trouble to couple together.'

'So do you,' I said. 'If you thought this was

183

just a motherly visit, why did you go on about Lady Edwina and all the...'

'Lady Edwina?' asked Mrs Knox.

'Yes,' said Bill. 'Daughter of Lord Tennerhill. Ever heard of him?'

'Tennerhill,' mused Mrs Knox. 'Tennerhill. Yes, I think so.'

'What I thought,' Bill said, 'is that there's nothing like example. We ought to present her with a pretty little picture of one of Marise's friends engaged to an eligible young man with an unimpeachable background.' He turned to me. 'Can you,' he asked, 'produce one?'

'Not a single one,' I said.

'I don't believe you try,' reproved Bill. 'Well, in that case I propose that Poopy and I should start the ball rolling and appear before Lady Edwina as a devoted young couple.' He looked blandly at Mrs Knox. 'Don't you feel,' he asked, 'that it would put us all on a firmer footing?'

Mrs Knox, for the first time in my knowledge of her, appeared a little at a loss. 'You sound to me,' she said, 'as though you're being rather flippant over a serious matter.'

'Flippant?' Bill's tone was injured.

'Flippant! Didn't you,' he asked Poopy, 'distinctly hear me use the word propose?'

'Yes,' said Poopy.

'Am I not,' Bill asked her, 'an indisputably eligible young man with an...'

'Yes,' said Poopy.

184

'And wouldn't we,' asked Bill, 'make a devoted couple?'

'My half would,' said Poopy.

'Bill,' began Mrs Knox appealingly.

'I ought,' said Bill, 'to have asked your permission. But I have here in my pocket, if you'd care to see it, her father's blessing. I also have in this pocket—no, this one—a rather expensive sapphire set in a little circle of diamonds.' He looked at Poopy. 'If you don't like it,' he said, 'I...'

'Yes,' said Poopy.

'Bill,' said Mrs Knox, and this time there was some anger in her voice, 'I would like...'

Bill leaned over, put out a hand, and patted her knee soothingly. 'There, there, there,' he said. 'Everything's all right. Everything is really quite in order. Don't you know that ever since she first saw me Poopy has loved me? Don't you know that after the first natural shrinkings of a confirmed bachelor I allowed myself to return her passion? I wrote to her father and I enclosed a check and a sketch of a ring. If he looked kindly upon my suit, I said, would he expend the check on a ring of just the kind shown herewith? Would you like to see it?'

'No,' said Mrs Knox, 'I wouldn't. A proposal, Bill, if this is one, is a thing which a girl should look back upon as something...'

'Sacred,' said Bill. 'I thought of that, but you must admit the difficulties. To make a sacred proposal, you must get the girl by herself.

185

Alone. Now the only time I see Poopy alone is when we're riding, and since I didn't fall in love until the monsoon broke, I should have had to propose in pouring rain to a girl in a wet mackintosh and sou'wester. She looks sweet in a sou'wester, but half the time she's riding ahead of me. How can I propose to the back of a wet sou'wester? And at home Poopy has two friends—two loyal and charming friends. They...'

'I'd have gone away before dinner,' I said, 'if you'd asked.'

'Could I propose to Poopy,' demanded Bill, 'with you knocking on the bedroom floor and saying "Can I come down now?" Could I go on one knee at the moment when Ali came in to fold the table napkins? Or when the second bearer brought in the finger bowls? Or when the third bearer came in with the olives and the salted almonds? Could I, Poopy?'

'No,' said Poopy.

'Do you,' asked Bill, 'mind a proposal that isn't sacred?'

'No.'

'Do you mind it in front of all these gaping people?'

'No.'

'If I got on one knee, Poopy, and said that I love you, which I do with all my heart, would you prefer it?'

'No.'

'Will you marry me, Poopy?'

186

'Yes. Thank you.'

'If you come here and sit on the end of my chair,' invited Bill, patting it, 'you can see the ring.'

Poopy sat on the end of his chair and Bill, taking a little box from his pocket, put the ring on her finger and bestowed the lightest of kisses upon it. Poopy held out her hand while we examined the stone and exclaimed at its beauty. Her face was turned to Bill, and my sister would have declared that there wasn't any expression on it whatsoever. But after one glance at it I looked hastily back at the ring, and when Bill put out a hand and took her free hand gently into his, I knew that he, too, had learned to read Poopy's face.

The remainder of his visit was rather confused. Congratulations on his engagement mingled with reproaches from Mrs Knox on the manner of its beginning. We all talked except Poopy, who remained seated on the end of Bill's chair listening to us and saying nothing.

Bill's departure and his farewell to his love were quite private, for Mrs Knox, Miss Brooke, and I remained in the drawing room while Poopy accompanied Bill into the hall. Here they could murmur to one another without fear of any intrusion. Only Ali, puzzled by Bill's prolonged farewells, stood by the front door, ready to usher out the guest, and Kariman, disapproving of Poopy's thin dress in the cold hall, shuffled out and insisted on putting a coat round her shoulders and, going back and forth at intervals, besought her to say good-by quickly to the Sahib and come inside.

Upstairs in our bedroom, Poopy and I talked, not of her affairs, but of Marise's. Poopy was happy. Poopy was engaged and her future had no longer to be speculated upon. But Marise—that was different. We talked of her and of Maurice, exchanging views as we undressed.

Poopy made a special journey from the bathroom, toothbrush in hand, to press home a point. 'You couldn't imagine Bill,' she said, 'ever having listened to anything his mother told him. I mean, he did, but it doesn't show now. You can see that at about fifteen or sixteen he began to do things in his own way—to be a man. But Maurice...'

'You've dropped the paste off your toothbrush,' I told her.

Poopy bent to retrieve it.

'I can't imagine Maurice ever standing up to anybody, any woman, I mean,' she continued.

'That's why I think Marise ought to marry him. She's never going to be the kind of wife who'll listen to what her husband says, and so it's just as well for her to get one like Maurice, who'll do what she says.'

'Poopy, you can't use that same bit of tooth paste,' I said in disgust. 'It's been on the floor.'

'It looks clean,' said Poopy, after examination. 'And I'm only going to spit it out again.'

She went back to the bathroom and I climbed into bed slowly, wondering what Marise's thoughts had been when she heard of Lady Edwina's proposed visit. She would tell us when she came in, but it was difficult to know how much of what she said was truth and how much, marble staircase.

After a few moments, I called an anxious question to Poopy. 'Poopy!'

'Hm?'

'Do you think Marise is really in love with Maurice?'

The sound of vigorous brushing stopped for a moment, and Poopy's voice came through the tooth paste. 'If she wasn't before,' she said, 'she will be now.'

CHAPTER SEVENTEEN

Marise's comments on Lady Edwina's visit began on a violent note and changed, after the first few outbursts, to acid reflections on her probable appearance and disposition.

Poopy allowed these two stages to pass. Only when Marise went on to discuss the details of her own plans for the visit did Poopy intervene. 'It's no use going on like that,' she said. 'A person can come and see her son if she wants to.'

'She wouldn't have wanted to,' said Marise, 'if she hadn't thought he'd been caught by a French minx with designs. Well, let her come. By the time she arrives she'll find her son engaged to the French minx.'

'No, she won't,' said Poopy.

'No? You think not?' asked Marise. 'If I wanted to be engaged today, yesterday, any day, I could have been. How many times do you think Maurice has asked me to marry him?'

'Nobody wants to know,' said Poopy. 'The point is you mustn't get engaged before she comes out.'

'No? And have no position, no standing at all? How silly you are, Poopy! When I'm engaged to him, I can say this and that to her and she'll have to take notice. If I'm not, then who am I? Nobody. She can talk to Maurice and make him listen to her, and he can't say, "No, I must ask my fiancée." I'm going to be engaged to him and...'

'No,' said Poopy, 'you're not. Not before she comes out.'

'Yes, I am.'

'Listen,' said Poopy. 'When you told me things to do with Bill I listened, didn't I?'

'Yes, but this is...'

'Well, then,' proceeded Poopy, 'now you can listen.'

190

Marise listened. During the weeks that elapsed before Lady Edwina was among us, Poopy and I had the privilege of watching Marise turn before our eyes from a self-assured, poised young woman into a halftone reproduction of herself. She gave up wearing ribbons in her hair by day and flowers by night. The shoes with long spikes for heels vanished and were replaced by simple shoes of the type worn by Poopy and myself. She took off the ten or twelve thin glass bangles which had jingled on one arm for the past month and gave them to Kariman. She discarded the dresses which, in the past, she had described as 'real French chic' and wore instead the dresses which had been made under our eye earlier in the monsoon. A slight, very slight French accent developed and Poopy let it pass. Even the little shrug, the occasional phrase in rippling French, was felt to be a helpful signpost pointing to her French ancestry. Poopy took away her nail varnish and bought her a polisher of the buffer type. I hid the enormous straw hat in which she had looked so beautiful. At the end of three weeks we were ready to face Lady Edwina.

Maurice became more and more happy as his mother's arrival drew near. His periods of leisure seemed to become more frequent and he was often in the house, outlining his plans for his mother's visit and looking at Marise with a glance in which there was love and pride and no shade of apprehension.

Lady Edwina was to live on the tea estate and not, as we had half feared, at a hotel in Darjeeling. Her visits would therefore be brief and in Maurice's company. She was to arrive on the following Tuesday and would be taken straight to Leboongi. On Thursday Maurice would bring her up to Darjeeling to call upon Mrs Knox and to meet Marise. She would stay overnight with us and return to Leboongi the following day. Maurice would be put up by Bill.

Immediately after lunch on Thursday I was obliged to hurry off to Miss Gumm, but my attention was scarcely upon music. I knew that Miss Gumm was giving an unusually impassioned rendering of a Brahms scherzo, and I understood that she was putting all she had into a subsequent performance of a haunting little Chopin mazurka. But I was longing to know what was happening at Landslide House. While Miss Gumm was searching her own pile of music to find some notes she had made for me, I was gathering my sheets from the music rest and cramming them into my case.

'Thank you. Thank you very much,' I said. 'Good-by.'

'It is nod dime,' declared Miss Gumm.

'Oh, yes. It's past the time, it's late,' I said earnestly, from the door. 'Thank you very much. Good-by.'

I was free. I was walking uphill as fast as I could go. I reached the house breathless, almost too breathless to run upstairs. There was nobody in the bedroom or on the balcony, but Poopy's voice came from one of the dressing rooms.

'I'm in here,' she said.

I threw my music case on the bed and went in to join her. To my surprise, I found a chair drawn up to the small window and Poopy kneeling upon it.

'Where's Marise?' I asked.

'She got a note this morning. Maurice asked her to go down, if it wasn't raining, and meet them at the top of the Leboongi road and then they'll all walk up here together.'

'That isn't a bad idea,' I said. 'Lady Edwina'll see her by herself. What're you kneeling on that chair for, Poopy?'

'I'm going to try and see them out of this window as they come,' said Poopy, craning her neck and peering out of the small aperture. 'I can see quite a bit, and they won't be able to see me. There isn't room for both of us, but I'll tell you what they all look like.'

'Did you see Marise go out?' I asked.

'No. Mrs Knox asked me to go down and invite Cloma to dinner. Her husband's here. He and Bill were at Harrow together. I had to ask them both—Cloma and her husband, I mean, and I stayed and talked for a bit. When I came back, Marise had gone.'

'What was she wearing, Poopy?'

'I don't know. I wish I did.'

'I wish I'd known,' I said despondently. 'I could have lent her my blue with the braid. It would have been absolutely the right thing and she looks so lovely in it. And it would have been simple and she could have worn your blue hat. Oh, Poopy, why weren't we here?'

'Here they are!' said Poopy. 'They're coming. I can see them.'

I stood on tiptoe but could scarcely see above the narrow sill.

'Tell me. Go on, Poopy,' I urged. 'What's Lady Edwina like? Does she look like Maurice?'

'She's tall and fair and quite good-looking,' said Poopy.

'Is Maurice in between them?'

'No. Lady Edwina's in the middle.'

'Are they smiling? Do they look happy?'

'I think so. I can't see their faces very well from here, but Marise just said something across to Maurice and they all laughed.'

'Oh, Poopy, do you think it's turning out all right? Does Marise look … Oh, if only we'd been here! She could have had the blue, with your blue hat. What's she wearing, Poopy?'

'Your blue,' said Poopy, 'with my blue hat.'

*   *   *

Dinner that night was something of a

celebration. Nobody knew what made it so. No blessing had been pronounced on the lovers; no word had been spoken about their future. But something was different. Perhaps it was our feeling that nobody could hold out against Marise's charm. She had rehearsed for weeks and was playing her part to perfection. Her manner to Lady Edwina was at once shy and friendly; with Maurice she was tender but reserved; with us she was gay and so natural that Poopy and I wondered nervously how long she could keep it up.

I had come downstairs with Poopy and Marise and thought that everybody looked very well-turned-out. We had allowed Marise to wear a small white flower in her hair. Her dress was new, close-fitting to the hips and billowing out into a wide, swirling skirt. Poopy was demure in white, and Lady Edwina wore a beautiful dress with what Bill spoke of in her presence as floating attachments. I had just come to the conclusion that we all looked as nice as it was possible to look, when Cloma walked in and shattered my complacency.

She was in a sari of pure gold cloth. Lady Edwina, who had an eye for values, fixed it upon the magnificent shimmering folds and could scarcely remove it again. Against her tall husband, clad in a conventional black dinner jacket, Cloma stood, a little golden statue.

When our eyes met, I saw a glint of amusement in hers. 'How,' she asked me in a

195

murmured aside, 'are things going?'

'What things?' I asked.

'Everything.'

'It was going all right before,' I said, 'but that sari has put the finishing touch on it.'

Bill was in the highest spirits. He called the slim Mr Vrishna Fatty and explained, at our protests, that Fatty, at fourteen, had weighed almost two hundred pounds.

'Isn't that so?' he asked him.

Mr Vrishna smiled. 'You ought to know,' he said. 'I sat on your chest several times.'

'Well, don't go into that,' said Bill. 'Do you know what this party's being given for?'

'For Lady Edwina?'

'Certainly not. It's an engagement party,' said Bill.

He grinned across the table at Maurice, and Maurice rose to his feet, glass in hand. 'I think we ought to drink,' he said, 'to a happy couple—Poopy and Bill.'

We drank and cheered and drank again, and Bill rose to respond. There was a sudden silence as he leaned with both hands on the table and looked round.

'This,' he said, 'is a very happy occasion. We are here to celebrate an engagement. We're here, in fact, to celebrate two engagements: Poopy's—and mine. I thank you all for your congratulations. But we have another toast to drink, a toast of welcome. There is a lady here to whom we all accord a hearty welcome. May she stay long and love us all very much. Ladies and gentlemen—Lady Edwina.'

I don't know whether it was the toast or what we drank it in or the general atmosphere of good will or Marise's beauty or the contagious effect of Bill's engagement, but when we got up from the table we all knew that Marise and Maurice were not going to find any obstacles in their path. They would marry. We couldn't, just after dinner, have given the date, but of one fact nobody was in any doubt. Lady Edwina had capitulated.

CHAPTER EIGHTEEN

Since it was a season of engagements, I was not surprised a week or two later to get a letter from my unattached sister telling me that she was engaged to a gentleman called, in block capitals, Thomas Kemp. I was relieved to find that I remembered him. He was the most athletic of all the young men and had played tennis singles with me on several occasions while we were waiting for my sisters. I was able to write and say that I thought him just the thing to improve my sister's backhand strokes.

We were nearing the end, I realized gloomily, of one of the happiest years I had ever spent. My most recently engaged sister was to be married in Calcutta in December.

The other was to be married in England in March. Close upon this news came a bombshell—my father was to retire in February. He might, he added, give way to pressure and come out for a further four years' service, but his present decision was to go home permanently early in the New Year.

Poopy was undismayed at this news.

'Bill and I,' she told me, 'are going to be married in England. Bill's mother's blind, and he wants to be married near his home so she can be at the wedding. You'll be three bridesmaids—one for your sister in December and one for your sister in March and one for us whenever it is. And if Marise could only make up her mind and hurry up, you could be four.'

It was Lady Edwina who made up her mind. She was to go home in December and wanted Marise and Maurice to marry before she left. It was arranged that the wedding should take place at the end of November.

I was, therefore, to be a fourth bridesmaid. Under any other circumstances four new dresses would have brought great solace, but it seemed to me that life, which had been so pleasant, was in process of being carved into unrelated pieces.

'But we're all coming back,' Poopy pointed out. 'Your father's sure to do the extra four years, and if he doesn't you can come out to me and you can come out to Marise, and there'll always be your sisters.'

I was thoughtful for a few moments and then put a question. 'Do you think,' I asked, 'that Marise will be happy living at a tea garden?'

'I don't suppose they'll live long at a tea garden,' said Poopy. 'They'll be able to leave it whenever they want to. Maurice isn't doing it for a living, exactly. I think myself that when Marise has a baby, Lady Edwina'll want it brought up in England.'

I was glad to hear that my father was coming up on a brief visit. His arrival was delayed, for the rains had brought the railway line down in several places and passengers had to walk from the rail end to a waiting train farther along the line. My father arrived too late in the evening to come and see us, but I walked down to his hotel early the following morning and led him in triumph to the house.

He was only up for ten days but he wanted, before going down again, to see Miss Gumm and get from her some idea as to the progress I was making.

'You mean you just want to see her?' I said. 'I shan't have to play, shall I?'

'I don't see why not,' said my father. 'That's what you go there for, isn't it?'

'Well, yes, in a way.'

Miss Gumm said that she would be delighted to see my father. We went on the afternoon appointed and found her in the music room. My father's eyes, searching among the trophies, came to rest upon the piano and he looked relieved.

'Sit down,' said Miss Gumm, indicating a sofa overlaid with a leopard skin and removing from it two magnificent boar's heads. 'Sit down, please. You have gone to ask of the young lady's progress?'

'Yes,' said my father.

'She is good. She blays well,' said Miss Gumm. 'She shall blay you something of what we have done together, and you shall see.' She swept aside an antlered head and rummaged among her music, producing at last a battered folio. 'This—the Chobin scherzo,' she decided. 'Come, blay.'

I seated myself at the piano. I like the B flat minor scherzo. It begins with a dash and goes on with a flourish. The performer has scope; there are fat chords to lean on and rippling passages to skim over; there are rich, satisfying harmonies. Miss Gumm liked it, too. Before I had got through more than the preliminary flourish, I saw her bearing down on me and prepared to vacate the piano stool.

'A little more emphasis!' she said. 'I will show you.'

She played it beautifully. She followed it up with an étude, which she assured my father I played extremely well. She ended with a brilliantly executed Bach prelude.

We thanked her warmly and she shook my father by the hand. 'She blays well,' she assured him. 'Very well.'

200

Walking slowly homewards, my father asked whether all my lessons were conducted on the same principle. 'Do you,' he asked, 'ever blay her anything?'

'Well, yes, sometimes. The first bars, anyhow.'

'I see. And do you find the method helpful?'

'Oh yes. After all,' I pointed out, 'she does much more than most music teachers. Most of them sit by your side and say "Thrum, thrum, thrum," but how many of them could illustrate as well as Miss Gumm? There's not much point, is there, in my doing at my lessons just what I've done at my practice? Most music lessons just work out as a practice with someone listening, but every time I go to Miss Gumm, she...'

'Gives a recital,' said my father. 'Well, I don't suppose you could attend a weekly recital for less. But wouldn't you get the same stimulus from records?'

'Records? But they wouldn't *look* like Miss Gumm. They wouldn't bend their ear down and...'

'No, they wouldn't,' agreed my father.

We hesitated at a turn of the road. We could go up or down. We went down a little way and sat on a bench where in clear weather there was a wonderful view. We sat in silence for some minutes. Presently I asked my father whether he was pleased about my sisters' engagements.

'Yes,' he said. 'A man's always glad to settle

201

his daughters well in life. They've both got hold of fine young men. Incidentally, your two young cronies haven't done badly either. It doesn't seem long since the little French miss was walking up our staircase in Minto Lane with that ayah padding after her, and Poopy was hitching up those pants of hers. I heard from old Colonel Melyard a month or so ago. D'you remember him?'

'Yes. I suppose he wanted you to retire in Shillong?'

'That's just what he did want.'

'Did you say yes?'

'No. It would be a good life—comfort, good climate, exercise, sport, lovely scenery. But when I finish here, I'd like to go and do a bit of fishing on the rivers I knew as a boy. But I'm not sure that I'm finished yet. You'll get a great deal more out here than you would if I retired. Your sisters are well settled, but I've got you to think about. I've...'

It struck my father at this point that he was seldom able to make so long a speech without interruption. He turned to discover what was keeping me so silent and gave an exclamation of astonishment.

Tears!

The phenomenon was so staggering that my father took a few moments to recover. Then he trod delicately in what he imagined was the right direction. 'You know,' he said gently, 'some girls take longer than others to ... well,

202

to meet young men they like. You're still very young, and ...'

'Men!' The genuine astonishment in my voice put my father at ease on at least one score. 'Men! I don't want men. There are a jolly sight too many men! I wasn't thinking about men. I was only thinking about us—all of us, Poopy and Marise and, well, everybody. Everybody's going away, everybody's going to be married, everything's going to be ... Well, nothing's ever going to be the same again.'

Here my voice was lost in snuffles and my father waited for me to recover. When I was in a position to listen, he spoke. 'Look here,' he said gently, 'I want you to answer a few questions. Will you?'

'Well, go on.'

'It isn't much; it's just to try to bring home to you how much you've had and to try and make you feel grateful for it. You were a nice comfortable trio, you and Poopy and Marise, but it was bound to break up in time, and you're wrong to think it's over. All you've had will remain in your mind throughout your life, a sort of firm base of happiness on which you can build. Good health, a happy childhood, a carefree girlhood—you've had them all and you can look forward to a happy and useful future, please God. You're going to see Poopy in the future, aren't you? She's not going completely out of reach?'

'N-no.'

'And you'll see Marise settled in her new home and visit her often?'

'I suppose so.'

'And in time you'll have a home of your own and try to give your children a happy start?'

'Perhaps.'

'You've had almost as much happiness in your life as countless people can reckon on in a long lifetime. Do you know that?'

'Well, yes.'

'And don't you feel deeply grateful?'

'Yes.'

'There you are, then,' said my father. 'Those tears were wasted. You haven't anything in the world to cry about. Here's a clean hankie.'

'I've got one.'

There was silence. We both looked straight ahead and thought our own thoughts.

'One thing,' I said at last, 'you'll have to admit. I'll see Poopy and I'll see Marise, but it'll never be quite the same again, will it?'

'Well, perhaps not,' said my father.

'And in time they'll be much more interested in their husbands, won't they, than in me?'

'Well, yes.'

'And in their homes and their babies?'

'Naturally.'

'So that all this—the happy childhood and girlhood and all—it's over. It's finished, and nobody knows what's ahead, do they?'

'True.'

'And however many friends I make, they'll

never be what Poopy and Marise were?'

'Well, no.'

'And whatever's ahead will be different, won't it? I mean, getting married is all right but it's responsibility, isn't it, and thinking about bringing up children, and it's never quite what you said—carefree—any more, is it?'

'Well . . . no.'

'And so everything *is* over, in a way, isn't it?'

'Well . . . yes.'

I rose and dusted off my skirt. 'That's what I said,' I said.

We hope you have enjoyed this Large Print book. Other Chivers Press or Thorndike Press Large Print books are available at your library or directly from the publishers. For more information about current and forthcoming titles, please call or write, without obligation, to:

Chivers Press Limited
Windsor Bridge Road
Bath BA2 3AX
England
Tel. (01225) 335336

OR

Thorndike Press
P.O. Box 159
Thorndike, Maine 04986
USA
Tel. (800) 223–6121 (U.S. & Canada)
In Maine call collect: (207) 948–2962

All our Large Print titles are designed for easy reading, and all our books are made to last.